Falling for a Smart Cowboy

VARGAS RANCH BOOK 4

Karen Baney

Falling for a Smart Cowboy: Vargas Ranch Book 4
By Karen Baney

Publisher:
Desert Life Media, LLC
Gilbert, AZ 85295

www.karenbaney.com

Printed in the United States of America

ISBN 978-1-960217-39-4

This is a work of fiction. Names, characters, businesses, places, events, and incidents are either the products of the author's imagination or used in a fictitious manner. Any resemblance to actual persons, living or dead, or actual events is purely coincidental.

With regard to the works of man,
by the word of your lips
I have avoided the ways of the violent.
My steps have held fast to your paths;
my feet have not slipped.

Psalms 17:4-5

1

_____

DEVON VARGAS STRETCHED out his long legs as he watched the sunrise from the secluded back patio of his parents' home. It was an unusually cool June morning for Arizona, only in the upper eighties. The forecast called for the low one hundreds by the start of the gigantic party Mami had planned for him.

Pink and orange painted the sky, casting a soft glow on the surrounding desert landscape. Towering saguaro cacti, their arms adorned with sharp spines, stood proudly against the horizon, their majestic presence a testament to the arid beauty of Arizona. At their apex, large white flowers blossomed, signaling the arrival of summer — a visual promise of the transformative monsoon season. Just one more sign of the changes in his life.

His leg bobbed a steady cadence as his boots created a soft tapping sound against the wooden deck. Restlessness wound around his heart. Despite the tranquil surroundings, he struggled to find calmness. He ought to enjoy the peace. What had Rennie said the other day? She advised him to slow down to savor the present moment, urging him to let go of his perpetual pursuit toward the next achievement. Stop striving.

Well, watching the sunrise counted, right?

Not really. Even in the serene moment, his mind raced over a dozen things. Hiring a director for the children's program before he left for Guatemala felt like the most pressing.

After the third children's director hired in a year left last month, Devon wondered if he just wasn't cut out to be a leader—not like his older brothers Dalton and Derin. There had to be something wrong with him, that these women kept leaving.

He snorted. The first one, Angel, had been married and expecting her first child, so he could not honestly blame himself for her departure. He just wished she would have let him know she hadn't planned to stay before he hired her.

Then there was Ava. Piece of work. Great with the kids, but scatterbrained as all get out. Developing the program required a certain level of organization that Ava lacked.

Devon cringed at his judgemental attitude. Ava didn't deserve his internal criticism. In truth, it came out of his frustration with himself. He hadn't had enough time to mentor her. She may have been able to learn it in time. Unfortunately, last fall, his final project for graduate school had consumed much of his waking thoughts and energy. That's why he hired Ava—to run the children's program at his family's guest ranch and resort.

The last attempt to find a children's director... He shook his head. It still chafed.

"*Mijo*."

Devon looked up at the sound of his mother's voice. He noticed the strands of gray in her dark hair as it framed her classic latina features—a heritage not visible in his own.

"I thought I heard someone pull into the driveway."

Her flip-flops thwacked softly against the deck as she walked toward him. The aroma of freshly brewed coffee wafted from the mug in her outstretched hand, along with the tantalizing scent of vanilla cinnamon creamer. He accepted the offered beverage, sipping it a few times before setting it on the small wrought-iron table next to his cushy patio chair.

"Are you excited about the party?"

Devon frowned. Mami knew he preferred not to be the

center of attention—at least not with adults. Leading kids, teaching them, encouraging them felt more comfortable to him.

"Your papi and I are so proud of you. Two degrees."

Devon let the words bounce off his heart. A bachelor's in secondary education and master's in instructional design were necessary for his goal to become a history teacher. He didn't see what all the fuss was about. It's not like he was the first son to achieve the milestone. Dalton sported an MBA from Arizona State University. Dylan earned a bachelor's in equine science at Colorado State University. Out of the four oldest sons, only Derin chose not to go to college.

Mami reached over and squeezed his hand, sighing loudly. "You must learn to celebrate the good things in life."

She released his hand and stared into the distance. "So much like your papi. He never…"

Though Devon said nothing as her words trailed off, they perplexed him. He was nothing like his easy-going, steady Papi. Surely, Papi had never been driven by some internal, insatiable desire to make his mark on the world. Devon could not explain where it came from, only that it nipped his heels at each accomplishment in his life—completely the opposite of his father and any of his four brothers.

His oldest brother, Dalton J. Vargas the fourth, exhibited the most similarities to his papi. Entrepreneurial. Devoted husband and father. Since marrying River and the birth of their twins, Sloane and Elena, Dalton continued to follow in Papi's footsteps.

Not like Devon. He couldn't wait to move off the family ranch. Go do something meaningful with his life, like the mission trip to Guatemala to work with children. Or like teaching history at a high school. Pour into the hearts and minds of the next generation, including sharing about Jesus, if the opportunity arose. If he liked the mission trip, he hoped to plan more during school breaks.

He cleared his throat. "Mami, I really need my birth certificate. I'm running out of time to apply for a passport."

"Oh, *mijo*! I thought I gave it to you months ago." Mami stood abruptly as her eyes shifted toward the house. "I better check on breakfast."

Before he could press her further, she whirled into the large ranch house. The sweet fragrance of her perfume lingered in the air. Devon sighed before draining his coffee. Then he entered through the back door.

Mami leaned down to open the oven. A blast of heat warmed his arm as he walked by. Instantly, the spicy aroma of Mami's *huevos rancheros* filled the air, reminding him how delicious the breakfast casserole tasted.

"Morning!" Dalton greeted him, pouring coffee into two large mugs. "Congratulations, Dev. Are you excited about the party?"

Why did everyone keep asking him that?

His older brother leaned against the counter, sipping the brew while he waited for an answer. When a baby's cries echoed down the hall, Dalton pushed away from the counter.

"Sloane is up. Be right back," Dalton said before scurrying from the kitchen, leaving the two mugs of coffee behind.

His grandfather, Padre, chuckled from his spot at the kitchen table. Devon never understood why they called him Padre, since the word meant "father" in Spanish. Not grandfather. Maybe because he was Papi's padre? He shook off his musings as Padre spoke.

"Reminds me of Tres when you boys were little. Always stealing moments with each of you."

When Padre glanced at him, a shadow fell over his countenance for a moment before he smiled. Something about Padre's initial reaction set Devon's nerves jittering. Ever since Padre revealed the dramatic family secret about the loss of their sister—a twin to Derin—last spring, Devon wondered if there were more skeletons in the family closet.

"Joining us for breakfast?"

"I just came to watch the sunrise. I'll grab something from the coffee shop before heading over to see if Dylan needs help to set up for the morning equine therapy session."

"They ended for the season yesterday," Papi said as he finished pouring himself a black coffee.

"Don't they usually meet on the first Saturday of June?" Devon asked, confused.

"Not this year. We've been planning your graduation party for months. Didn't want to split focus away from you."

Mami placed a turquoise trivet on the center of the table. Yes, like many random facts, Devon knew what a trivet was. Papi donned the oven mitts and carried the casserole dish over to the table. When he removed the oven mitts, Papi placed his hands on both sides of Mami's face before kissing his wife. Devon thought it might have been a little too heated for first thing in the morning, and in front of their son.

He wondered for half a second what it might be like to love someone that deeply for so long. They had to be nearing the forty-year mark soon, given Dalton's age of thirty-six. Then Devon remembered he didn't have time for love right now. At twenty-six, he still had plenty of time for it. Later. Much later.

"Coffee?" Papi asked, raising the pot after he filled a mug for Mami.

Devon shook his head. Papi came over and squeezed his shoulder. His father's blue eyes searched his.

"Stay. Have breakfast with us."

Devon sighed as Mami set a tall glass of orange juice on the table for him. Guess he wasn't getting out of it. Sitting next to Padre, he studied his father. Papi's blue eyes matched Derin's. Not Devon's green ones. Dylan and Drake shared Mami's chocolate brown eye color. Though Dalton's gold eyes differed from their parents, they were a replica of his *abuela's*. No one had green eyes. No one save Devon. Not even his cousins.

Why he suddenly noticed these things, he could not say. They bothered him all the same. He may have started paying more attention after Padre's slip up about their late sister.

When River, Dalton's wife, padded into the kitchen, she propped Elena on her hip. Her long blond hair piled on the top of her head in a messy bun almost out of reach of her daughter. Elena's blue eyes lit up when she spotted Devon. Could she be old enough to recognize him? He held out his arms, offering to hold his nine-month-old niece. As he gazed lovingly at her, he marveled at how soft and squishy she looked. He let her grab his finger, and she rewarded him with a drooling gurgle. Goodness, he loved the little bug.

The next generation of Vargas children had finally arrived with the birth of Dalton's twins last December, Sloane and Elena. Dylan and Brisa were expecting their second child in August. It surprised Devon that Derin and Madison had announced no children on the way yet. Their first anniversary was only a few weeks away. The two had been inseparable since Madison moved to the ranch.

Devon studied his family as Mami handed out plates. The dark circles under Dalton's and River's eyes seemed less pronounced compared to a few weeks ago. The twins must be sleeping for longer stretches. He caught Dalton studying his wife and noticed the look of adoration. Yeah, each of his older brothers had fallen deeply in love.

When Elena fussed in his arms, River took her from Devon. Within seconds, Sloane joined in. River excused herself to feed them both. A smile tilted the corner of his mouth. She had really taken to motherhood, just as Dalton had become a doting father.

A longing tugged at Devon's heart. Strange. He had not felt this before. This curiosity about fatherhood. He had no time for such longings. He hadn't even started his new career yet. Hadn't announced he planned to leave the ranch for good.

The clanking of silverware following the prayer pierced his conscience. He ought to tell his family about his plans. But first, he really needed to hire a children's director. One that could run the program and make his absence from the ranch less noticeable.

RAINA CRAWFORD PULLED onto the dirt and gravel drive of Vargas Guest Ranch & Resort just outside of Wickenburg, Arizona. A Saturday interview date still confused her. The resort manager, Renata Vargas, confirmed the date and time by email again yesterday.

As she parked in front of the office, she blew out a slow breath. This job had been made for her. Children's programming director at the family run resort on a guest ranch. Kids and horses. Nature and amenities. Could it be any more perfect?

Raina glanced in her rearview mirror, relieved to find her curly hair had not frizzed up. The drier Arizona climate seemed kinder to her natural curls.

After exiting her beat up old Ford Focus, miraculously still running after the long drive across multiple states, she ran a hand down the length of her modest skirt, smoothing out any wrinkles. Doubt crept in. Perhaps a skirt seemed too professional for a job working with children. Oh well. It's not like she would start today if hired.

As she scanned the area, the sun warmed her back. The bright yellow paint on the resort office building popped against the natural backdrop of desert mountains striped with multi-colored striations. Gold, rust, white, brown. The bright blue sky stretched overhead from horizon to horizon. Not a cloud in sight. The perfectly manicured plants brought pops of lilac, orange, and gold, softening the bleakness of the desert. She breathed deeply, enjoying the sweet fragrance in the air, wondering which plant it came from. She wouldn't mind living in such a beautiful place.

When she stepped toward the office door, she frowned. The lights were off. Then Raina tried the door. Locked.

Glancing at her watch, she still had a few minutes before eleven. Perhaps Renata would arrive shortly. Or her husband Devon. From her phone conversation, it sounded like Renata managed the resort and her husband managed the kids' program. Raina envisioned a sweet middle-aged couple. Entrepreneurs, judging by the expansive property. From the turnoff on the highway, it took her another ten minutes to reach the place.

This job would provide the critical experience Raina needed for her goal. Having survived the foster system since her tenth birthday, she longed to open a program for middle school foster kids. She wanted it to be a place they could come to experience unconditional love and acceptance. A safe-haven. A glimpse of what life could be like. Something to give them hope for their future. Just like the loving couple who taught her about Jesus.

She had only been with them for three months. She had been eleven or twelve. In the sixth grade, if she recalled the timing. After her parents died, Raina had been shuffled from group home to foster home to group home again. Mostly, she tried to hide. Fade into the background and let the rowdy kids take the brunt of any harsh treatment by the adults.

She did not know how she had ended up with the Radcliffs. She only remembered how, for those brief months, she felt treasured. Loved. They told her about Jesus and how He loved her. Wanted to walk beside her no matter what life threw at her. No matter where she found herself.

When the social worker tore her away from the older couple, dropping her into another group home, Raina wailed the entire car ride. The pain in the couple's eyes told her they truly had loved her as much as they said. Life became much harder after that. She learned how to protect herself. She remembered to talk to Jesus when alone. Raina had survived solely because of the hope she found in Jesus and with the Radcliffs. It had been enough to save her.

Only now, in her mid-twenties with a college degree to her name, did she feel like she was becoming her real self—the woman God designed her to be. She may not have any close friends. She may have rarely experienced love from adults growing up. But Raina Crawford had been filled with the love of her Savior. She could give love to the kids that crossed her path. She could bring them hope. And maybe, just maybe, she could be a Radcliff to the hurting children God placed in her path.

Raina puffed out a breath of air. Except she first had to win this job, learn everything she could, become the best, and save up money to start the refuge she dreamed about. With God on her side, it would come to pass. She knew it deep in her soul.

The blistering sun warmed her skin to almost searing, rousing her from her wistful thinking. Sweat beaded at her hairline before her wild, curly mane absorbed it. Raina glanced at her watch again. Quarter after eleven. She sighed and trudged back toward her car, disappointed the interview did not happen.

A man's deep voice boomed over a speaker, muffled by the walls of the building next door. Raina veered toward the sound, pausing at the double door entrance long enough to notice the sign: "Closed for a private event." For a few seconds, she debated about entering what must be an air-conditioned room. When sweat trickled down her back, she yanked the door open, desperate for relief from the summer heat.

Her face flushed as she realized she had stumbled into some sort of celebratory party. The smoky aroma of BBQ wafted toward her, causing her mouth to water. Perhaps she could snag a bottled water before driving back to the hotel to try again on Monday.

"Madi and I are pregnant!" The deep voice sounded over the speakers.

The people swarmed the giddy man and the stunning blond standing next to him. Hugs and congratulations mixed with tears of joy. Smiling faces surrounded the lovely couple. What would it be like to have someone in her life care for her like that?

Raina's eyes roamed the room. The decorations didn't fit with a gender-reveal or baby announcement. They were more subdued, like that of a graduation party. Yet, no one wore a cap and gown. In fact, most of the men wore western-style shirts, jeans, and cowboy boots. The women's outfits ranged from flowing maxi dresses to western shirts and jean shorts. She had never met a friendlier-looking crowd. A pang of homesickness—for the home she never had—threatened to further dampen her mood. She quickly stuffed it down.

As she continued scanning the crowd, her eyes landed on the most heavenly pair of green eyes. Eyes like hers, only not as bright green. The breathtaking cowboy wore a solid olive green shirt, neatly tucked into the trim waist of his deep indigo jeans. His simple brown belt with a plain silver buckle stood out compared to the ostentatious buckles of the other men. Brown wavy hair flopped over his creased forehead. He seemed annoyed by the couple's announcement.

Just then, his head lifted, and his gaze rested on her. Raina swallowed down her fear as his eyes caressed her hair, her cheeks, her nose. That she could almost physically feel his scrutiny unnerved her. It shouldn't. There was something pure and reverent about it.

When the cowboy pushed away from the wall, ambling toward her, Raina considered darting out the door. She was trespassing. Clearly, the smart-looking cowboy reasoned she did not belong. But she could really use a water and that BBQ smelled divine.

Squaring her shoulders, Raina swallowed down her fear like she had a thousand times growing up. Then she straightened her back. She flipped her curly hair over her shoulder and pasted a smile on her face, ready to fake her way through the next few minutes.

2

"MADI AND I are pregnant!"

The high-pitched feedback from the mic hurt Devon's ears, and he frowned. Of course, his older brother stole the spotlight. It should not surprise him. The opening of the celebration had started a half hour ago, with Papi and Mami calling him up to the makeshift stage. They gushed with words of praise for his achievement. So he should not be upset with Derin. He had waited for a convenient pause in the celebration to deliver the exciting news. Instead, he ought to join the throng swarming his brother and his wife. Another Vargas child on the way.

Devon's dour mood irritated himself. He should be happy. Celebrating his accomplishment. Instead, he slinked to the back of the crowd at the one event about him, the fourth son, eager for his chance to leave.

Normally, Devon did not crave attention. In truth, the attention today still unsettled him. At an intellectual level, he knew the significance of completing his master's degree. He even took pride in it.

Receiving his family's praise had always been hard. Today had been no different. It would be better if his inability to accept their congratulations came from humility. It didn't. He felt unworthy. No matter how much he succeeded in life, he still felt lacking something inside. He shouldn't. Devon knew Jesus died for his sins. Believed He loved him. He served in the children's ministry at church out of that love.

Devon shook his head as he looked down at his feet. There was something seriously wrong with him.

When he lifted his head, his gaze tripped over a beautiful woman. Her wild, blondish-brown curly hair framed her silky skin like a puffy monsoon cloud. He wondered if it was as soft as it looked. Her green eyes widened slightly as he studied her features. His eyes locked onto hers again. Across the room, he caught her flicker of fear before she replaced it with guarded confidence. A smile twitched at the corner of his mouth.

Devon strode toward her swiftly—not because he wanted her to leave his party. Quite the opposite. He felt drawn to her. Like the siren's song in the Odyssey, the mystery woman pulled him to her.

As he neared, he reminded himself to smile. No need to frighten the mesmerizing creature away.

"This is a private party," he said, keeping his voice light.

"I saw the sign."

He nodded, taking in her professional appearance. Pristine ivory blouse. Crisp dusty rose pencil skirt. Perfect legs. Even with the high-heeled wedge sandals, the top of her head barely met his chest. The thought caused heat to spread over his face as he looked down at her beautiful countenance. Those bright green eyes. For several seconds, he became lost in them.

"Are you a friend of the guest of honor?" she asked, waking him from his bizarre stupor.

"No."

A dark blond eyebrow arched high over one of those enchanting green eyes.

"We have plenty of food. Have you eaten?" he asked, ignoring her unasked question, preferring to invite her into his world. Why? Well, that was a mystery to ponder another time.

"I could eat. I would love some water, too."

Devon led her toward the buffet line. As he passed Dalton's wife, River, he heard her ask, "Since when does he have a girlfriend?"

He held back a chuckle, amused by the thought. Him. Devon Vargas with a girlfriend? And one bold enough to crash his graduation party? Not likely.

Though he wanted to pry about her unexplained presence at his party, he chose not to. He would much rather stay in her orbit just a little while longer.

"Do you live in the area?" he asked as he piled his plate full of the smoky pulled pork. His mouth watered at the aroma.

"Hopefully."

Odd. Based on his observation, he concluded she was a newcomer. Despite the town's small population, he wasn't familiar with all of Wickenburg's residents. If he had met her before, he would definitely remember by now.

His guest took a small amount of pork and chicken before filling her plate with salad. Sometimes he wondered if women really wanted to eat that many vegetables. He certainly didn't.

"And you?"

"I live on the ranch."

She nodded slowly as she scanned the room for a table. When Devon touched her elbow lightly, she jerked harshly away, causing her plate to loosen from her grip.

"Sorry," he said reflexively, as the salad smashed into his shirt. His favorite shirt. Those lovely green eyes rounded in disbelief as she appeared to almost fold into herself.

"I'm so, so sorry." Her voice sounded smaller, meeker than before. Maybe tinged with fear. That made no sense.

Working with kids taught him not to sweat the small stuff. Like having food dumped on him. He had certainly worn worse things over the years. Mud. Honey. Glue. And that unidentified substance little Matt, one employee's son, ground into the carpet and all over Devon's arm. Took him the better part of a day to clean it off his hairy arm.

When the woman's lip trembled, he ducked down to meet her gaze, sensing the need to diffuse the situation. Using his calming voice, he tried to reassure her no harm had been done.

Just then, Rennie appeared next to him. "I'll clean this..." Her hand clamped over her mouth as her eyes rounded. "Oh, no! Please tell me I didn't?"

Rennie withdrew her phone from her back pocket, tapping and swiping frantically before she let out a tremendous groan. By now, several other family members gathered around. Mami scooped up the plate and food from the floor. Drake already wheeled a mop and bucket in their direction. River started another plate for the mystery woman. And Rennie shook her head.

"I totally told you the wrong date," she lamented.

The curly-haired siren finally found words—words which took a few seconds to register in Devon's confused mind.

"Pardon?"

"I'm Renata. And this is Devon Vargas. And I'm so sorry I scheduled you for Saturday. I meant Monday."

The woman's face turned bright red before she muttered something under her breath, rushing out the door.

"Who is she, Rennie?" he asked, as his cousin hurried behind her.

"Raina Crawford. The perfect candidate for the open children's director position."

Devon held the door open as Rennie scurried toward the woman, stopping her before she slid behind the wheel of her car. Devon swallowed hard as his mind processed everything that had just happened.

Raina was there for an interview with him. He couldn't let her get away. Especially not if she turned out to be as perfect as Rennie claimed.

RAINA'S EYES BURNED as the horror of her mistake flashed before her like a digital billboard on the side of the freeway at night. She should not have come for the interview until Monday. Of course. No one interviewed on a Saturday. What had she been thinking?

Worse yet, she dumped her meal all over the resort manager's husband. The man she would report to. She hadn't expected his light touch on her arm. Her instincts from her formative years had kicked in. Flight became her overwhelming goal.

There went the perfect job. The job she had spent three days driving to get to. Parking her car at night in a well-lit parking lot, trying to sleep in it in strange cities. She arrived in Wickenburg last night. Found a cheap motel so she could at least shower and primp a little before donning her only professional outfit for the interview.

The interview scheduled for Monday. Not today.

The tears spilled over as Raina ran from the building. *Lord, I really wanted this job. In this nice place. It looks safe. Wonderful. Help me get over the disappointment of my failure.*

"Wait, Raina!"

Renata Vargas's voice stopped her as she reached for the handle of her stupid piece of junk car.

"This is completely my fault. If you're willing to wait a minute, I can get you the application."

Raina snorted. "Sure and I suppose your husband will still want to hire me after I threw my lunch on him?"

Renata's brow wrinkled as Devon's voice came from just outside of her peripheral vision. "I work with kids. Projectile vomit, paste, and even honey are harder to clean up than a little salad."

When Raina looked up at him, he offered a smile. "If you'll give me a minute to change my shirt, I'd be happy to interview you today."

"Devon, it's your graduation party," Renata said, biting her lower lip.

"Rennie, she came all this way. I can skip an hour of my party."

Raina's chest squeezed tight. The party was for him? How much worse could the day get?

"Give me ten minutes, then bring her back to my office."

Raina blinked at his back. His wonderfully broad shoulders. She quickly scolded herself for being attracted to another woman's husband! She ought to jump in her car and drive away. Far away. Like to California or something.

By the time Renata escorted her to the office, Devon had unlocked it and disappeared behind a dark wood door.

"Would you care for some water?" Renata asked.

Raina nodded numbly as she slid into a chair. "I'm sorry about your husband."

Renata snorted. "Devon is my cousin. My single cousin who just graduated with his master's degree."

Raina inwardly breathed a sigh of relief. At least she hadn't been staring at a married man. Still, her instant awareness of him had her wondering if it would be wise to stay. The last thing she needed was a romantic relationship. She had a mission, a purpose. A handsome cowboy didn't fit into her plan.

Her pulse settled as Renata asked her to fill out the application. She scratched out her meager employment history and references, slipping a copy of her resume under the application. Then she sipped her water as she handed the clipboard back to the young woman, probably around the same age as Raina.

By the time Renata led her to Devon's office, through the children's center, Raina regained her confidence. She could do this. Maybe.

A row of large windows ran along one wall of the children's center. Neat hip-high shelves lined the space beneath them, filled with clear bins holding toys for different age groups. Raina noticed the order, youngest to oldest, left to right. Fabric-covered partitions created a cubby in one corner of the room where several beanbag chairs and a low couch sat. That must be a space for preteens and teens. She supposed the resort guests included children of all ages.

In another section of the room, a rug with the image of roads and trees laid next to softer interlocking mat pieces in primary colors. A portable pen sat on the far side. Raina could envision little boys pushing plastic cars along the road rug and toddlers pounding blocks against the softer mat.

An unexpected jolt of sadness rose inside her, causing her eyes to burn. Kids were amazing, resilient. As much as she hoped to have her own one day, she knew it was impossible. Still didn't take away the longing.

Now was not the time to wallow in her heartbreaking reality. It didn't matter, anyway. She would not allow herself to fall in love because loving someone meant they had the power to break your heart.

Raina cleared her throat before straightening her back and holding her chin high. She needed this job so she would think good thoughts instead.

Renata led her into Devon's office, closing the door as she left.

"Please have a seat," Devon said, motioning toward one of the cushioned chairs across from his small Scandinavian desk, which seemed out of place — too modern for a ranch.

As Raina took the offered chair, he shuffled papers on his desk. She squared her shoulders, releasing a soft sigh before smiling.

"Early childhood development degree. Impressive."

She held back a snort. He had no idea. She had worked hard for a scholarship and to complete the degree in three years, instead of the traditional four. Summer classes had been the only way to provide a roof over her head.

Shoving the thoughts away, Raina expanded on his

comment, highlighting her qualifications and her approach to program development.

"Older children frequently attend the center, too," he said. "Though if they are high school age, we usually send them with Adan for outdoor activities—horseback riding, ATVs, and more."

"Do the girls like that?"

"Eh. Some do. He's a good-looking former pro bull rider, so there's that." Devon scoffed. "Some just want to read a book."

"I can write up a plan for crafts and low-key options for teens who prefer a quieter day."

Devon's lips stretched in a smile. "That'd be wonderful."

"If you don't mind me asking, what's your degree?"

Red colored his cheeks and neck as he glanced away. "Secondary education and instructional design."

"Oh." Odd choice for running a place like the children's center. Raina kept the thought to herself.

"I'm currently applying to teach high school history in the area."

"You mean you will not continue to work here?"

"No. The position you're applying for is to take over my job."

Raina blinked, suddenly overwhelmed by the responsibility. She had hoped he would be a mentor.

"I'll train you through the summer before I leave for a mission trip to Guatemala. Then I'll be here for a week or two before the school year starts."

She let out a stuttered breath.

A frown formed on Devon's face, making Raina feel a wave of discomfort. No matter how hard she tried to appear calm, the rapid heartbeat and shallow breaths betrayed her nerves. With her lower lip caught between her teeth, a strong sense of dread settled in, convincing her she was on the verge of losing this job.

"Will that be a problem?"

"No. Not at all." She lied. She really wanted to learn from him. Of course, she had also thought he was middle-aged and married, too. Her assumptions had been all wrong.

It made no difference. She needed this job. And the room and board listed on the ad so she could stop living out of her car.

Raina flashed her most charming and confident smile, hoping he could not sense her fear. "When do I start?"

3

ON SUNDAY MORNING, apprehension filled Devon as he headed over to the cowboy church early. He still couldn't believe he had hired Raina for the children's director's position. She was younger than he expected. He had hoped for someone with a few years' experience. Raina couldn't be over twenty-four, if that. And her reaction when he mentioned she had applied for his job? Not confidence inspiring in the least. Hopefully, he could train her in the next six weeks.

His shoulders sagged as he climbed into his 4Runner. He had too much to do. Still needed to find someone to take over with the kids at church. Train the pretty new director. Finalize his passport application. Devon groaned. He must tackle that first thing tomorrow. Greg was counting on him for the Guatemala trip. All that training would be for naught if he didn't get a passport.

The side lot was empty as Devon parked his car, the only sound being the crunch of gravel under his tires. Stretching to his full height, he breathed in the morning air. The sun beat down on his face, already intense. The forecast predicted a scorching day, and the relentless heat was already making its presence known. Before arming his vehicle, he carefully tucked his phone into the pocket of his shirt.

When he rounded to the front of the church, he stopped short. Raina Crawford sat on the steps, with her curly hair barely tamed into a fluffy ponytail, which reminded him of a rabbit's cotton tail. She wore a light blue t-shirt that said, "I may not be perfect, but Jesus thinks I'm to *die* for." A smile twitched at the corner of his mouth. Her jeans flared at the bottom, where a pair of light brown combat boots peeked from under the hem.

Devon failed to keep his eyes from traveling the length of her as she stood. Even on the middle step, she still stood a few inches shorter than him. Her green eyes lit with pleasure as a sweet smile spread across her pink lips. All his words fled as a vision of kissing her flitted through his mind. Heat inched over his face as his gaze shifted to the wall behind her.

"Morning! Pastor didn't mention you were in charge of the kids' program at church."

Devon shook off his wayward thoughts. "For now."

"I'm here to help."

"Middle school?"

She nodded, and her ponytail barely moved. It hung suspended in the air, frizzy and immovable. Kinda like the cotton candy they served at the harvest festival in the fall.

"Put me to work."

Devon held the door open for her before leading her down the side hall toward the middle school room.

"How was the room?" he asked.

"Oh, it's amazing. I'm not used to having so much space all to myself."

His head jerked to the side. Thankfully, she walked in front of him, missing his bewilderment. The women's dorm rooms were small. At least that's what his cousins whined about. Often.

"What time do the kids arrive?" she asked as she ran a hand along the shelves full of books and toys.

"Usually about ten minutes before service starts. Sometimes as much as fifteen minutes after."

Raina giggled. "Sounds about like my church back

home."

"Omaha?" At least that had been the address listed on her resume.

"Yup. Except we had two services, so I usually served during one and sat in the other."

"We're not big enough for that. I usually watch the recording of the service in the afternoon."

Devon showed her around the room and where the restrooms were. Inevitably, one or two kids needed to use the facilities during the hour.

As he set out props for the lesson, Raina scanned the books on the shelf. Selecting three, she set them on the top of the bookshelf.

"What's the plan, Devon?"

The warmth that spread through him at her use of his given name confused him. He had never reacted to a woman like that before. It was only his name, for goodness's sake.

"I prepared a small lesson. Then we have an activity."

"Is there time to read them a story?"

When she caught her lower lip between her teeth and looked at him through her lowered lashes, his heart melted. He'd make time for it.

"Sure."

As her face brightened, his mood lifted. Why her joy made him happy wasn't a thought he cared to examine for too long.

A half hour later, with the lesson and activity completed, he took a seat on the floor, joining the circle and looking forward to Raina's storytelling. It was evident from her first sentence that she possessed a gift for it, captivating her audience with every word. Beyond just reading, she performed the story through seamless transitions between voices and changing her facial expressions to match each character. The kids' eyes remained glued to her, and they eagerly requested another when she finished. It was like watching the pied piper, her charismatic presence drawing everyone in.

She would be great with the children at the resort. And in Guatemala, even if she wasn't bi-lingual like him. The thought of her going on the trip with him brought heat to his face.

"Mr. Dev?" One little boy named Austin patted Devon's knee.

He leaned over, giving the boy his full attention. Austin danced back and forth, and Devon figured the boy needed to use the restroom. He stood to his full height and offered his hand to Austin. When Raina quirked a brow, he mouthed "restroom." She nodded once to acknowledge him.

"Let's go."

Austin tugged his arm, so Devon hastened his steps. When they reached the restroom, he waited outside the stall for Austin.

"Wash your hands," he reminded the boy before they walked back down the hall.

The last notes of a familiar worship song filled the air, along with the aroma of freshly brewed coffee. The music faded and the pastor's voice rang out with a closing prayer. Devon scooped Austin into his arms, propping him on a hip as he hurried back to the classroom, arriving seconds before the first parent came to retrieve their kid.

For the next fifteen minutes, Devon greeted each parent, introducing Raina. Several of the children hugged her before chattering to their parents about her storytelling. A smile tilted the side of his mouth. The last of his doubts about the cute young woman disappeared. She would be a great addition to Vargas Guest Ranch & Resort.

"Mijo!" His mother's singsongy voice preceded her entrance into the classroom. "I heard you had a new helper today."

"Mami, this is Raina Crawford. She's the new children's director I hired yesterday."

Mami clucked her tongue. "You should not have made her come out on a weekend."

Devon shrugged off the chastisement, opting not to explain the situation as Mami engulfed Raina in a hug. Her frizzy ponytail barely moved, despite his mami's animated embrace.

"Welcome, *bonita*! Join us for *cena familiar*."

Raina's head angled toward her shoulder.

"Family supper," he quickly explained.

"Oh, I couldn't impose."

Mami threaded her arm through Raina's and gently nudged her toward the door. Raina planted her feet and turned toward him, green eyes locking on his. She was so pretty in a girl-next-door way. And why he kept noticing was beyond him.

"Do you need help to clean up?"

Devon glanced around the room. "Looks like you covered it already."

He laughed as Mami ushered Raina out of the classroom, as he straightened the last few chairs. No surprise that Mami adopted her already. Then he flipped off the lights and closed the door behind him.

Guess he'd get to know Raina better at supper. For some odd reason, the thought put a spring in his step as he headed out to his car.

RAINA EXTRACTED HERSELF from the kind Mexican woman's grip as she listened to her directions to the Vargas family home. After she repeated them back, she hopped in her car and drove there.

As she rounded a bend in the dusty road, the sight of three immense homes came into view—the third, almost twice the footprint of the other two. Suppressing the urge to let her jaw drop, she switched off the engine, taking in the scene. A mix of excitement and wonder washed over her, making her heart race as she absorbed the grandeur before her.

The massive home blended well with the scenic backdrop of the desert. The mountains in the distance appeared almost purplish in hue, fading to the light tan of the desert floor. Short trees with green trunks and bright yellow flowers provided color to the otherwise overwhelming earth tones. The light yellow painted stucco of the home appeared almost gold in the shadow of the sweeping front porch. A huge dark green door with a frosted glass insert beckoned to her.

Raina could not imagine what it must have been like to grow up in such a beautiful home on an expansive property. Wanting for nothing. Surrounded by God's majestic creation. That old familiar longing for home threatened to morph into the scene before her. This was not her home. It would never be her home. Fairytales never came true, not for someone like her.

A light tap on her window pulled her from her thoughts. Devon's perfect white teeth gleamed in the sunlight with his smile. Warmth bloomed on Raina's cheeks as she grabbed her purse from the seat while he opened her car door.

"You have a beautiful home," she said, nervously fiddling with her keys.

"Thanks. I don't live here anymore. I have a bunk in the bunkhouse. But hopefully this fall I'll get my own place."

She matched his strides up the porch stairs while a little boy trudged along the ramp she hadn't noticed earlier. His light brown hair bounced with each step. He wore tan cargo shorts and a bright blue t-shirt. A gap-toothed grin split his adorable face as he hurried toward them on the metal prosthetics. Raina's breath lodged in her throat and she placed a hand over her heart. He had no legs!

"Uncle Dev!"

"Hey, Braden," Devon said as he crouched down, holding his arms wide. "Sporting the blades today?"

Braden giggled as he launched himself into his uncle's arms. Devon's arms folded around the kid before he stood and spun him around.

"Let me down!" Braden said between infectious giggles.

Raina's eyes burned at the sight. The tall, handsome man had a gift with children, endearing him to her even more. He would be a wonderful dad. The thought brought heat to her face again. She ducked her head to hide her embarrassment.

When Devon set his nephew down, the little boy ran into the house. Raina bit the inside of her lower lip to keep from asking about the boy's legs.

"He lost his legs in a car accident three years ago. Guess we're all used to seeing him run around. I forget it's unusual. He's my brother, Dylan's adopted son. His wife's from a previous relationship."

Adopted. Something she had coveted for years until she finally accepted it would never become her reality. How many nights had she cried herself to sleep asking Jesus to bring her a new mommy and daddy? Her eyes burned, and she blinked rapidly.

"You okay?" Devon whispered as he reached toward her. At the last minute, he dropped his arm, stuffing his hand in his pocket instead of touching her. She wondered if he remembered her reaction to his touch yesterday.

Raina cleared her throat and squeaked out a "Yeah."

Devon studied her for a few more seconds before he spoke. "My family is pretty big. You ready for this?"

"Your mother seems very nice."

Devon led her through a massive great room to a bright kitchen teeming with activity. A blond woman held two babies, one on each hip, bouncing them up and down. A man almost as tall as Devon took the one wearing blue, while somehow handing the woman a bottle.

"That's Dalton and River and their twins, Sloane and Elena."

Raina smiled and whispered a greeting as the couple left

the kitchen.

Devon introduced her to a man with very broad shoulders and another blond woman. She recognized them as the couple from the party who announced they were pregnant. Derin and Madison. Madison promptly shooed Derin out of the kitchen after the introduction.

Another woman glanced up from the salad spinner. Devon called her Brisa and mentioned she was Braden's mom.

"Ah. Dylan's wife."

Before she knew it, Raina found herself caught up in the flurry of meal preparations. Brisa, who had taken Raina under her wing, introduced her to Renata's sister and mother, who were also lending a hand in the kitchen. Devon excused himself and left the room.

Catalina greeted her again as she handed her a bowl for the salad. Brisa slid lettuce into the giant bowl and Raina added the veggies she had been chopping.

The tantalizing scent of spicy Mexican food wafted through the kitchen, filling the air with its aromatic allure. Raina's mouth watered in anticipation, her senses captivated by the delicious aroma. She could almost taste the delectable flavors that awaited her.

As the aroma of the delicious food filled the dining room, each woman carried her carefully prepared dishes to the table. Catalina graciously directed Raina to take a seat across from Devon, positioning her between two of his sisters-in-law. Surprisingly, everyone remained standing, causing Raina to find the situation rather peculiar. However, she stood still, waiting for the reason behind this unusual behavior to unfold. Then Catalina's husband, Tres, led the family in a moving prayer, thanking God for family and friends and sharing a meal together.

Suddenly, every person around the table raised their voices. "We do not deviate from the Lord's plan. Amen."

The hairs on Raina's arms stood on end as the sound of

chairs scraping across the tile floor filled the room. She hesitated, still awestruck by the words the family prayed together. River encouraged her to sit before she explained.

"It's the Vargas family motto. It takes some getting used to. The family recites it at every shared meal to remind us that God is in control and that we serve Him."

Raina's throat constricted, so she reached for her water. God had been so good by bringing her there. Providing a job. But this... This family was an astonishing blessing, far beyond what she could have asked for or imagined. It had been less than twenty-four hours since she arrived on the ranch, and yet their love for each other was so strong she felt it already.

She listened to the conversation humming around her, observing the interactions almost as if she was on the outside looking in. Some of Devon's brothers teased each other. Others asked about the week. The women asked how she was settling in. Their sincere interest struck her. It soothed the open wound in her heart to know someone cared, if only as an acquaintance.

When her gaze snagged on Devon, she noticed him lean forward, waiting for her answer. Raina answered his question and tried to deflect the other questions about her. The unwanted attention of everyone made her uneasy. Fading into the background had been her survival mechanism for too long.

When it hit her, she sucked in an audible breath. This. This was what an actual family looked like. The overwhelming flood of emotions snuck up on her. A sob tore from her throat and Raina jumped to her feet, rushing through the kitchen and out the back door, struggling to pull air into her lungs.

She had waited her entire life for a family. People who cared about her. People to pray for her. How very fortunate Devon was to have so much love and support. Why couldn't she have grown up with a family like his?

"Why, Lord?" The question fell from her lips like a feather.

Raina knew it was pointless to ask why she never got to experience the love of a family. No adoption after countless tear-filled prayers. Always longing for the simple security of a home, a place to belong.

She leaned against the coarse stucco of the house, feeling its rough texture against her back. Slowly, she slid down to the wooden floor of the back deck, the coolness of the weathered wood seeping through her clothes. Tucking her knees up to her chest, she buried her face in her hands, feeling the weight of her sorrow consume her. Old memories lingered in the air. Overwhelmed, she sobbed, her cries echoing in the quietness of the surroundings, releasing the pain of her shattered childhood dreams.

4

"MIJO, GO!"

DEVON craned his head and widened his eyes at his mother, his curiosity piqued. He eagerly awaited an explanation for her unexpected command.

"Vamos!"

Taking a deep breath, he stepped outside into the hot midday air. The sun cast intense light against the wood decking. His mind still swirled with confusion, unsure of why Mami insisted he go after Raina. Rennie or River, any female, would be better suited for this task.

As he walked, he uttered a quiet prayer, seeking guidance in this uncertain situation. He couldn't deny the nagging sense of unease that lingered within him.

Squinting against the bright sunlight, he scanned the patio. Huh. Maybe she left.

Just as he started to head back inside, Devon heard the muffled sound of crying. He walked toward it. There, on the other side of the patio furniture. Raina sat with her back against the house, sobbing into her knees. His chest tensed.

With newfound resolve, he stepped toward her, ready to support Raina through whatever heartache she faced. He shuffled his feet noisily against the wood decking. Then he sat down beside her.

"Raina."

Though her cries quieted, she remained frozen, giving

no sign she heard him.

Devon prayed silently for wisdom. Then he looped his arm around her shoulders, easing her against his side. The warmth and softness of her body felt perfect. Such a foreign feeling—he did not know what to do with it. He redirected his thoughts back to praying for Raina.

After another minute, she lifted her head. When she looked up at him, she balanced herself by placing her palm flat against his chest. His breath and pulse quickened as he stared into her lovely green eyes. Her body flinched with a suppressed sob, tearing at his heart. He softened his features and rubbed his hand on her arm.

He ought to ask what bothered her, but words disappeared as rapidly as they attempted to form. For some inexplicable reason, Devon wanted to fix whatever had hurt this beautiful, innocent woman.

"What's wrong?"

At last, his whispered words fell into the space between them.

Raina sniffed and straightened, swiping away the dampness on her cheeks. "I'm sorry."

Then she lurched forward, about to bolt. Devon's hand clasped hers, stopping the motion.

"Stay. Talk to me."

She eyed him warily for nearly a minute before expelling a loud breath. Then she sank back against the house, leaving a few empty inches between them.

"I. Was. An orphan." Her voice quivered, accompanied by a shaky breath swallowed up by the large open space of the patio. A half-sob escaped her lips, causing her body to tremble. The faint scent of loneliness hung in the air as she whispered, "I never had a family."

Devon coughed to mask the emotion rising within him. He couldn't help but feel a pang of sympathy for Raina. She deserved to experience the love and loyalty that comes from having a supportive family. People always rooting for you.

Challenging you. Only because they wanted the best for you. No wonder she darted from the room.

She turned those red-rimmed green eyes on him again. Without a thought, Devon lifted his hand to cup her silky cheek. Using his thumb, he brushed away a fresh tear, his heart aching on her behalf. Raina held his gaze for several seconds, making him wish he could fold her in his arms. Rest her head against his chest. Breathe in the sweet scent of those soft curls. The air thickened between them, almost like it did right before a monsoon storm broke free from the skies. His eyes dropped to her full pink lips, and he leaned toward her siren song.

Then she launched to her feet, hugging her arms tightly around her waist. Her head bowed as she kicked the foot of a patio chair. As she looked anywhere but in his direction, his heart squeezed tight.

"I should go. I'm going. Tell your family I'm sorry. I truly appreciated the invitation. But I need to go."

Before he uttered a sound, she dashed inside. A minute later, he heard a car engine start, and gravel crunching under her car tires.

Devon sat there for a solid five minutes, puzzled by what happened. He almost kissed Raina. It was only yesterday when they first met. He was her boss, her employer. Running a hand through his hair, he heaped condemnation on himself. He was some kind of idiot, nearly taking advantage of a hurting, pretty woman.

"Dev?" Drake's voice sounded from the back door.

Devon stood and expelled a loud breath, shoulders sagging.

"Everything okay?"

"Raina had to go." Because he was a jerk. He figured it was best to keep that to himself.

"Mami will be sad to hear it. She thinks you like her."

Devon's gut twisted in knots. "I just met her yesterday."

Drake laughed, his dark eyes sparkling. "You know

Mami."

Devon couldn't argue. He knew Mami wanted him to marry, especially since his oldest three brothers brought such amazing women into the family. He had no interest in a relationship for a few years, didn't he?

Drake entered the house and held the door open for Devon. The flurry of activity in the kitchen gave him pause. He would have waited outside longer had he known.

Mami's gaze speared him while she handed a few empty plastic containers to Rennie. Rennie scooped huge portions of leftovers into one.

"I'll make a plate to take back to Raina," she said.

Devon nodded sharply, pleased Rennie cared about her new roommate. Mami placed a hand on his arm, drawing his attention.

"*Mijo*, do you want some?" Her eyes flicked between him and his brother.

Drake shrugged, and Mami thrust two filled containers into his hand.

"Take some for the cowboys if you don't want any."

"Si, Mami."

Devon filled a couple of containers, too. Sometimes he liked to eat the leftovers later in the evening instead of venturing out to the dining hall. He had no doubts that the other container would be gone by morning, especially if he marked it as fair game. The cowboys never turned down free food, especially if it came from any of the women in his family.

As he started to leave, he turned back to his mami, remembering the whole passport thing.

"Mami, I need to talk to you before I take off," he said.

"What is it, *mijo*?"

He jerked his head toward the living room, and she followed.

"I really need my birth certificate to finish my passport application."

Mami's faced shadowed. "Didn't I give it to you?"

Devon frowned, his gut twisting. "Mami, I don't have it. You know how organized I am. I wouldn't lose something like that. Especially not when I've been planning this mission trip for over a year."

Mami's dark eyes darted toward Papi, who gave a sharp nod. She let out an exasperated sigh.

"I'll bring it to your office tomorrow."

"Catalina—"

"Tomorrow." Mami cut off Papi.

Devon wondered what that was all about as he leaned down to kiss his mother's cheek. "Gracias, Mami."

When she placed her hand on his cheek, he froze, the hair on the back of his neck standing on end. His suspicion ratcheted to high alert over her unusual gesture.

"*Te quiero*, Devon."

He studied her face for a moment before he said, "I love you, too, Mamacita."

Mami held his gaze for another second, before stepping back.

Why was she acting so weird?

"Tomorrow, then," he said as he walked toward the door. He waved to the rest of his family before ducking out the front door.

His mother's odd behavior niggled in the back of his mind. Not knowing the reason for it, he turned his concern into prayers, asking God to be with his mami.

A SOFT KNOCK sounded from Raina's bedroom door. She held back a groan as she rolled over before sitting upright.

"Raina? I put a container of leftovers in the fridge for you." Renata's voice came from the other side of the door.

Raina's eyes welled up with tears as she forced herself to

swallow down her overwhelming sadness. With heavy steps, she trudged towards the door, the weight of her emotions dragging her down. As she reached out, her trembling hand gripped the cold doorknob, its metallic touch sending a shiver down her spine. With a creak, the door reluctantly yielded to her, emitting a high-pitched squeak that echoed in her room.

"Thanks."

"Anytime." Renata started to turn away, but angled back. A flash of sympathy crossed her features. "You want to talk?"

Raina sighed as anxiety contracted her shoulder and neck muscles. How long had it been since she trusted someone enough to confide in them? Yet, Renata was technically her boss as the Resort Manager. Dare she blur the lines between professionalism and friendship? Maybe it would help to talk.

At length, she finally said. "Yes. No. I don't know."

"I don't mean to pry. Just offering to listen. Or to put on a chick flick and grab a pint of ice cream from the freezer."

Raina snorted. "That sounds good. Only I haven't made it to the store yet."

"No worries. You can have one of mine. If you like vanilla caramel."

Raina followed Renata into their shared kitchen. The women's housing held four small bedrooms for each shared kitchen and living area. Besides Renata and Raina, Solana lived there. As she had just learned at the Vargas family dinner, Solana was Renata's sister and they were the cousins of the five brothers.

She sniffled as she accepted the pint of ice cream and a spoon. Imagine. Five brothers. Two cousins. Parents. Grandparents. Aunts. Uncles. All to care about them. So far from the lonely existence she had lived after her parents passed away. No extended family to take her in. No adoptive parents or siblings. Just Raina, and eventually her relationship with Jesus.

Confiding in another person ought to be alright. Unfortunately, Raina wasn't ready to let someone else in—not even a little.

As she flopped down onto the soft couch, cushions enveloping her in a comforting hug, Renata flipped on the TV and navigated to a streaming service. Raina ate a bite of the sweet ice cream, savoring the coolness on her tongue. When Renata suggested a sweet romance movie from the Hallmark channel, Raina agreed, glad for the cover for her cleansing tears.

The sorrow in her soul never seemed to disappear completely. It was a constant presence, lurking just beneath the surface, ready to emerge whenever she had a moment to reflect. No matter how much she tried to bury it or distract herself, it always resurfaced. It weighed heavily on her heart, casting a shadow over her thoughts and emotions. Even in moments of joy or laughter, a twinge of sadness lingered, a reminder of the pain she carried within.

She really ought to be grateful for all God had given her instead of wallowing. Grateful for things like this new job, a roof over her head, and her degree. There were so many people even less fortunate than her. Lacking a loving family, though it hurt, was not such a bad thing compared to what some people went through.

So why did it seem all-consuming, rearing its ugliness at the most inconvenient times?

As the couple in the movie declared their undying love for each other, Raina chose prayer over sorrow.

Lord, thank you for the Vargases. For this job. Help me to let go of the past. Live in the now. Turn my heartache over to you.

Raina set the empty ice cream container on the coffee table and snuggled deeper into her corner of the couch, letting the next movie distract her. One day, she would learn not to allow herself to covet what others had. She would learn not to take the good in her life for granted.

5

ON MONDAY MORNING, Raina woke feeling refreshed. She showered before the two Vargas sisters rose. Then she donned a bright pink t-shirt with the faded logo of some shoe company. Her thrift-store jeans fit perfectly, despite a stain near the waistline. She stuffed her feet into the brown combat boots. She knew they seemed like an odd choice of footwear for working with kids. Yet, they were so comfortable. She could stand for hours in them. And they lasted much longer than the last pair of tennis shoes she found.

She stared at her reflection in the mirror before applying a light dusting of powder, mascara, and neutral lip gloss. A soft sigh escaped her lips as she fluffed her difficult-to-control curly hair. Not much point in pulling it back. Mostly, it stayed out of her face.

Raina grabbed her purse and headed out to her car. Renata mentioned that most of the employees drove the mile to the dining hall, resort office, and children's center. She parked in a spot behind the building, next to a silver 4Runner. The back door of the children's center looked propped open a few inches, so she entered from there.

"Close it behind you, please." Devon's voice sounded from his office before he entered the main room. He wore a pair of charcoal cargo shorts and a heather gray fitted t-shirt with a sports team logo on it. When he flashed her a calm smile, her pulse quickened. He extended his arm, palm open.

"Here."

She accepted the shiny brass key from his hand.

"You'll need this to open and close the center." His green eyes sparkled with mirth. "Hadn't expected you so early."

Raina shrugged. "I wanted to get familiar with the place. Also, I figured you have some new hire paperwork for me to complete?"

"Come on back. We'll start with that."

He held his office door open for her and she sat across from his chair.

"Do you have two forms of identification?"

Raina dug in her purse for her driver's license and birth certificate. She resisted the temptation to look at her parents' names. No sadness today. It was the first day of her new career.

"I need to copy these." Devon headed toward the door to the resort office.

She filled out the other paperwork while she waited for him to return. When he did, he handed back her identification.

"Let me know when you want to take time off to get an Arizona driver's license and plates."

"Will do."

Devon set the copies and other paperwork face down on his desk.

"Ready for the grand tour?"

Raina followed him out the front door of the children's center. After he asked her to lock the front door, to make sure the new key worked, she followed him around the property.

"You remember the dining hall?"

"Yeah." Like she could forget dumping her lunch on him. Heat warmed her cheeks. Thankfully, he seemed not to notice.

"Some parents pick up their kids for meals. For those that don't, we take the kids around eleven-thirty. Chef sets out a few special items for them, like chicken nuggets and mac-n-cheese. If they have special dietary requirements, you or one care worker will need to let the chef know. I usually just send him a text by ten."

Raina made a mental note to set a reminder on her phone.

"We have four care workers during peak season. They have rotating days off, so we usually have at least three on site each day. Also, Renata's sister, Solana, occasionally helps if anyone calls in sick. She works at the front desk, but I'll make sure you have everyone's phone numbers. I have a group text setup for emergencies."

"Got it."

"Did you eat breakfast yet?"

"Not yet."

"Follow me."

When Devon held the dining hall door open for her, Raina caught the manly scent of his cologne. Smelled like cedar wood and pine. Her face heated as she brushed past him, breathing the pleasing scent a little deeper.

She scanned the large space, noting the gorgeous view of the mountain from a wall of glass windows. Hinges between the glass panels made her wonder if they could open up the entire wall to the outdoors, similar to pictures she saw of a lanai once.

Wood tables of various sizes dotted the room, each surrounded by wooden chairs. The buffet table had wheels on the bottom. Clever. Probably made it easier to rearrange for big parties. Like the one she had crashed.

"Morning, Raina!" Drake greeted her from behind the coffee bar with a smile.

Though she met him at the family meal the day before, she noted his man bun, black fitted t-shirt, dark denim, and black and white pin-striped apron. The cowboy boots were the only sign he worked on a ranch. Otherwise, he looked like he could work at a biker bar or coffee shop in any town.

"Employees get one free coffee on their first day and a nice discount after that. What can I fix for you?"

Raina smiled. "I'll take a vanilla latte."

"Iced?"

She shook her head. "Naw. I know it's weird, but I like hot coffee even in the summer."

"One hot vanilla latte coming up. Since we aren't busy, I can bring it out to you."

"Thanks."

Devon ordered a steaming cup of freshly brewed black coffee with a splash of vanilla cinnamon creamer. As the rich aroma filled the air, Raina couldn't help but conceal her smile. The beverage perfectly complemented the persona she associated with the cowboy.

She followed him over to a buffet with chafing dishes full of delicious smelling breakfast food. Devon handed her a plate, which she accepted.

"Breakfast, lunch, and dinner are all included for employees."

"All three?"

"Yup. Anything except the items from the coffee shop."

"Gotcha."

Gratitude bubbled up inside her as she plopped a spoonful of scrambled eggs onto her plate. She took a few pieces of turkey sausage and a yogurt before she found a seat at a table.

With all the drama of her first day in the dining hall, Raina hadn't noticed the family motto and verse stenciled over the dining hall doors.

She read the verse silently to herself. *With regard to the works of man, by the word of your lips I have avoided the ways of the violent. My steps have held fast to your paths; my feet have not slipped.*

And then the motto: *We do not deviate from the Lord's plan.*

The words settled over her heart. No matter what she had endured growing up, God had a plan for her life. Maybe more than one. Huh. Raina resolved to look for His plan even in the temporary while she earned enough to start the children's center of her dreams.

"Mind if I sit with you?" Devon asked.

"Go ahead."

He held out his hand, and Raina placed her palm on his large, smooth one. Tingles radiated from the touch, bringing warmth to her cheeks as she closed her eyes for Devon's brief prayer. When he released her hand, she grabbed her fork and stabbed a piece of sausage. Drake set her coffee and Devon's on the table. She thanked him.

"What's the story behind that?" she pointed to the family motto with her fork.

Devon smiled. "Family legend has it that my great-grandmother stenciled the verse above the door before opening day in 1952."

"Wow. That long ago? But why? What's the significance?"

Devon blinked and chewed a bite of bacon slower. "Huh. I don't know that I've ever asked. It's just always been that verse and the motto. We've repainted it several times, modernizing the font."

"It seems to me there might be something behind the 'I have avoided the ways of the violent.'"

"I think great-grandma picked it because of the part about 'my steps have held fast to your paths.' Both she and great-grandfather were always very devout Christians. At least according to Padre and Papi. They were gone long before I was born. But now you've made me curious. I'll have to ask."

Raina shrugged. "If you find out, you'll have to share it with me."

"Will do."

Throughout the rest of the meal, Devon told Raina more

about the job. Then he glanced at his watch and said they needed to go.

Even though no guests had booked for the week, a few children showed up at the center, including Braden, Devon's nephew. Today he sat in a wheelchair with a tan dog pulling it. The curly coat of the dog reminded Raina of a standard poodle.

Another kid, a few years older, introduced himself as Matt, one of the other worker's kids.

Raina spent some time with Matt and Braden getting to know them. She discovered Matt liked to draw. So she set out some drawing paper and pencils for the boys. Once Braden wheeled up to the table, his dog, Scout, found a spot in the corner nearby.

A loud noise from Devon's office sounded right before his door slammed shut. She told the boys she would be right back.

After knocking on the door, Raina eased it open, shocked by what she saw.

DEVON ENJOYED SITTING with Raina at breakfast. She asked brilliant questions and instantly won both Braden and Matt over. Next week, he expected a few more kids, though nothing like what they normally had during the peak season in the fall and winter.

Seeing the copy of Raina's identification on the corner of his desk, he walked over to the resort office. Once inside Rennie's office, he opened a file cabinet drawer. It surprised him that Rennie hadn't modernized their new hire process yet. He figured there must be online programs for storing new hire paperwork. Oh well.

Devon grabbed an empty file folder and neatly wrote Raina's name on it. Then he stuffed the paperwork in the folder and shoved the drawer shut.

An idea dawned. Surely, he and his brothers' information should be on file, too. Crouching down, he open the drawer with the v's and flipped through them. Dalton, Derin, Devon. His fingers froze as they grazed the tab with his name on it, his heart hammering fiercely. He shot to his feet and paced the small space.

Suddenly, sweat beaded on his forehead. His pulse raced. Why did it feel like he was doing something wrong? It was his employee file. He was part owner. He could read it.

Devon bent over, yanking the file from the drawer before taking it back to his office. He set it on the top of his desk, palm pressed against the front of the manilla folder.

He had lost count of how many times he had asked for his birth certificate. Mami had stalled. There was no other way to interpret her supposed forgetfulness. His Mami would give her sons anything — often before they asked. So why the delay with this? Why not just hand it over yesterday when he asked in front of Papi?

Swallowing down his fear, he opened the folder. He turned over page after page until his eyes snagged on the copy of his birth certificate. He scanned the names on it.

Devon J. Vargas, Jr.

His name. Junior?

Shaking his head, he reread the name. It made no sense. He was a fourth son. Papi's given name was Dalton, like his oldest brother. Not Devon.

His mouth went dry as he read the name on the line marked "father". Devon J. Vargas, Sr.

As he lifted the paper from the file, his hand shook. His eyes darted to the birthdate. It was his. Right month. Day. Year. Devon's hand shook so violently, he dropped it. The frightening paper fluttered to the stack inside his employee file. His heart pounded so hard he could almost hear it.

Then he read his mother's name. Anita Vargas. Not Catalina.

His parents weren't really his parents.

All the air whooshed from his lungs as he launched to his feet. He hurried back to the file cabinet in the other room. He grabbed Drake's folder and scanned for his younger brother's birth certificate, too.

Parents: Devon J. Vargas, Sr. Anita Vargas.

Devon dropped Drake's file back in place, slamming the file cabinet drawer shut, as if it was the drawer's fault for the secrets it held right under his nose all this time.

His throat constricted as he returned to his office. He paced the length of the room, trying to make sense of what he had just read. Green eyes that no one else had. Mami's comment about being so much like his papi when he was nothing like the man he called Papi.

The only logical explanation must be the truth: he and Drake were not sons of Dalton and Catalina Vargas. Their parents were really named Devon and Anita Vargas.

Devon shook his head as his stomach churned. An ache started to pound in his temples. He slumped in his chair, propped his elbows on the desk, and rested his head in his hands.

Who were Devon and Anita Vargas? Why hadn't they raised him and Drake?

Was this why Mami dodged his every attempt to get his birth certificate? She had known.

He snorted at the ridiculousness of his thought. Obviously, she knew she was not his birth mother — she had not given birth to him or Drake.

Drake. This would devastate him. He had always been so close to Mami. He would not take this news well.

The air whooshed from his lungs as the truth pierced his heart. He had grown up believing a lie. They both had. A huge lie. His relatives had raised them. Mami and Papi had covered it up. Hidden the truth from him and Drake their entire lives. Why?

Anger pulsed through his veins, and he shot to his feet

again. How could they lie to him for twenty-six years? Everything he thought he knew about them—was it all a lie?

Devon swiped his arm across his desk, violently shoving the files onto the floor. A guttural growl ripped from the depths of his soul. He felt betrayed. Hurt. And utterly alone.

A glimpse over his shoulder reminded him there were children in the adjoining room. He crossed it quickly, slamming the office door shut, causing it to rattle against the frame.

Who were Mami and Papi? Grandparents? Aunt and Uncle? What?

"Devon? Is everything okay?"

Raina's soft voice came from the doorway. He spun around and immediately regretted it when she shrank away. He closed his eyes, forcing his fisted hands to loosen as he filled his lungs slowly. After he released the breath, he opened his eyes again.

"What happened?" she asked.

Devon's shoulders sagged as he plopped down into his office chair. "I just discovered my entire life is a lie."

The sardonic words dripped from his mouth as he propped his elbows on the desk and rested his head in his hands. His eyes burned, and he bit the inside of his cheek to stem the threatening tears. The last thing he wanted to do was to cry in front of Raina.

The soft sound of ruffling papers came from the other side of his desk. He remained frozen in place, utterly embarrassed by his lack of control, first of his anger and now of his sorrow. Devon pinched the bridge of his nose, still hoping he could stop his eyes from leaking.

He glanced up right as Raina set the files and papers on the corner of his desk.

"I'm not sure what papers belong in which folder."

"Thank you. I'll take care of it later."

"Do you want to talk?"

Devon wiped a hand over his face as he drew in a sharp

breath. "Yes. No. Maybe?"

Raina puffed her cheeks. "I said the same thing to Renata yesterday."

"Ah."

Though he appreciated Raina's offer to listen, he needed to get out of the confining office. Talk to someone he trusted. Dylan.

"Thanks for... Think you can handle the kids for an hour?"

"Of course. It looks like Josh and Amber are here."

"Good. They can answer your questions."

As Devon stood and rounded his desk, Raina exited to the children's center. Then he hurried out the other door, through the resort lobby and outside before walking towards the stables.

Though Dylan was seven years older than him, they had always been close. Surely Dylan remembered something. He would have been seven or older by the time Devon came to live with them.

As sweat beaded on his forehead, he groaned. He probably should have driven over instead of walking in the summer heat. Oh well, too late now.

After fifteen minutes, he finally arrived outside of the barn. Dylan's truck sat in his usual parking spot. Good. He hadn't considered what he would have done had he not been there.

Devon eased open the door to the stable and allowed his eyes to adjust to the dimmer light. He listened for sounds of Dylan in the alleyway. Hearing nothing, he headed toward Dylan's office.

When Devon neared, he slowed his steps, studying his older brother—or cousin? They shared a similar squared jaw. A ring around Dylan's dark hair hinted that he had ridden earlier in the morning. Darker hair than Devon's.

He had been the lankiest of the Vargas brothers. This never bothered Devon before, as he spent far more time indoors than the others. Drake and Derin both had broad shoulders and beefy muscles, though Devon often wondered where Drake's muscles came from. Maybe running the dining hall and coffee shop involved more physical effort than he had considered. Dalton and Dylan, though not as beefy as Derin, were bulkier than him. Yet, Drake was much shorter than the other four.

Ugh. Looking for familial similarities twisted him up inside.

Dylan looked up. "Dev?"

"Got a minute?" he asked as he stepped into the office, closing the door behind him.

"Sure." Dylan turned away from his computer screen and gave Devon his full attention. "What's on your mind?"

"All settled in the new house?" he asked, deflecting to a safe topic. He needed to work up to the hey-I'm-not-really-your-brother conversation.

"I think so. Brisa is excited to work on the nursery. This weekend, we put together the crib."

"How does Braden like his new room?"

"He loves it. It's bigger than the room at the old house. I'm just glad the builders finished everything before the baby arrives."

Devon flashed a strained smile, knowing how much Brisa looked forward to Mami helping with the baby after its birth. Dylan and Brisa's brand new single-story ranch-style home sat between the family's ranch house and Derin's new home.

"What are you going to do with the old house?"

"Rent it out." Dylan dropped a stack of papers on one corner of his desk. "But I'm guessing you didn't stop by to ask about the house. Water?"

Devon nodded. Dylan leaned over and grabbed a bottle from the mini fridge in the corner. He handed it to him.

After he accepted the bottle, Devon's gaze darted to the corner of the room. His gut knotted, and he wiped a hand over his face as he let out a stuttered breath. He knew he had to gather his thoughts and find a starting point. The weight of the situation hung heavy in the air, and he could feel the pressure building inside of him. He twisted the cap off the water and took a long swig before setting it on a coaster.

"Do you remember when I came home from the hospital as a baby?" He held back a cringe, doubting his choice to start with his birth.

"Hmm." Dylan rubbed a hand along his jaw. "No, I don't. I remember when Drake was born. I would have been around ten years old then."

Devon exhaled loudly, then blurted, "I found my birth certificate."

"Oh? Did Mami finally give it to you?"

Devon shook his head. "I found a copy of it, I mean. In my employee file. It says…"

Dylan's head tilted to one side, eyes filled with concern.

"My parents are Devon and Anita Vargas."

He watched, waiting for the weightiness to hit his older brother. He noticed the moment it did. Dylan sat up straighter and brushed his hands across the top of his desk. Dylan's Adam's apple bobbed. His eyes pinched shut as he started to speak.

"N-n-not Dalton and Catalina?"

Devon shook his head. "Nope. Same for Drake. Drake and I share parents. I checked his file, too."

A shadow fell over Dylan's face as he muttered, "Devon and Anita…"

When Dylan looked up at the corner of the room, Devon waited patiently. He could see his brother's wheels turning.

"Aunt Anita. Uncle. Uncle Devon."

"What are you saying?"

"Dev, I think your father was Papi's…" He visibly swallowed as his eyes rounded. "Brother."

"That means you and I are —"

"Cousins."

Devon slumped back against the chair as nausea rolled over him. Mami and Papi were really his aunt and uncle.

"Oh! I remember," Dylan said. "You and Drake came to live with us right after he was born."

"What happened?"

"I… I don't know. I remember Papi gathering us boys together, telling us we had two new brothers now."

What did that mean? That his parents had abandoned them? Died? What?

Dylan shook his head from side to side, deep creases in his brow. "I'm sorry. I remember nothing more."

"Maybe Dalton does." Devon rubbed his hands on the top of his thighs before he stood.

Dylan cleared his throat, drawing his attention again. "Dev, talk to Mami and Papi about it."

Devon frowned. "Why? They've lied to me for my entire life. Why should I trust them?"

"That's not fair. You don't know what happened or why they brought you into our family as their own."

Devon scoffed.

"I'll pray for you," Dylan said as Devon stalked out the door.

He did not know what to think or say or do. So he headed back to work to clean up the mess he had made. If only the one Mami and Papi made could be cleaned up so easily.

6

———————

AFTER THE SECOND sleepless night in a row, Devon knew he needed to talk to his parents. He kept silent to Drake about the discovery, not wanting to throw him into a tailspin until he learned the truth. Even then, he wasn't sure he wanted to be the one to reveal it.

The bizarre dreams still perplexed him. A woman with green eyes and curly light brown hair. Not Raina. Yet, the woman felt familiar. When he closed his eyes and shut out his whirling thoughts, he could almost hear her voice reading him a bed-time story or singing softly over him.

Could she be Anita? His mother?

Devon growled and shoved open the door of the bunkhouse, stepping into the early dawn morning. He yanked his truck door open before sliding behind the wheel. His shoulders bunched and his stomach churned.

Work. Work would distract him.

Except he still needed his real birth certificate so he could submit his passport application. After wasting another week, he really needed to move on it today. Otherwise, he would miss the trip and let down his friend.

Instead of driving toward the dining hall, Devon turned onto the lane to the family ranch house. He parked outside, relieved to see both Dalton and River's trucks gone.

When he nudged the front door open, he announced himself.

"Mijo!" Mami—er, Aunt Catalina—called out as she entered the great room, wiping her hands on her apron. When she saw his face, she halted, her smile shifting quickly to concern.

"Tres! Devon is here."

Papi entered the great room, ushering Mami to a seat and motioning Devon to sit. He did as instructed.

"Look, I know I'm not your son," he ground out the words.

"Mijo! That is not true. You are our son."

"Mami... Do I still call you that? Or Aunt Catalina?"

"Son." Papi's tone and the stern set of his jaw left no room for argument. "You are our son."

"But I saw a copy of my birth certificate. I know the truth."

Devon folded his arms over his chest as his papi exchanged a look with his mami. Several seconds passed before Papi spoke.

"You, Devon Vargas, Jr., are our son. Adopted as one of our own."

"But I'm not your son, am I?" Nothing Papi said shed any light on what had happened. His heart rate catapulted as his breathing shallowed. When his lips parted, his papi—er, uncle—continued.

"Did we ever treat you or Drake differently from your brothers? Who taught you how to ride a horse? Take care of cattle? Listened to your bed-time prayers? Your mother wiped away your tears and kissed your owies away. She drove you to school and helped you with projects. So, you see, you are as much of our son as Dalton, Dylan, or Derin."

Devon narrowed his eyes at the couple who had been his parents as long as he could remember. Through gritted teeth, he asked, "What happened to my parents?"

Mami's eyes glossed with unshed tears. *"Mijo."* She leaned forward and placed a hand on his knee. "Your mamacita passed away when Drake was born. A complication during delivery."

When Mami sniffed, Papi cleared his throat. "Devon, Sr., your father…" Papi's eyes teared up, and he coughed. "He had been deployed to Afghanistan. Part of Operation Enduring Freedom."

Devon's throat constricted and his palms sweat. He uncrossed his arms and dropped his hands in his lap.

"Devon was the middle son. I was the oldest. Then Devon. Then your uncle Diego."

"What—" Devon's voice broke. He cleared his throat. "What happened to him?"

"He was killed in action. He had come home on leave for a few weeks. Spent time with you and Anita." Papi snuffled loudly before he crumpled into a fit of tears. Mami rubbed a hand on his back and continued the story.

"He went back. It was three weeks later he and his unit… None of them survived. He passed before he learned about Drake. Leaving your mamacita a widow."

Devon's hands trembled uncontrollably as raw, uncontainable emotion coursed through him. The weight of his father's loss in the war and his mother's tragic death during childbirth or soon after, bore down on him relentlessly.

The caged feeling forced him to his feet, desperate to put space between him and his parents—adopted parents. The urgent need to flee propelled him toward the door.

"I need my birth certificate, Mami. Today."

"*Mijo!*" Mami called after him.

He ignored her attempts to keep him from leaving. He brushed past her and hurried out the door. After climbing into his 4Runner, he shoved it in gear and drove toward the off-road trail by Dalton Peak. He couldn't go to work yet.

Dead. His birth parents were dead. Gone before he turned four.

Devon's eyes stung as his heart fractured within his chest. He eased his vehicle to the side of the dirt road and jammed the shifter into Park. Then he dropped his head back against the rest, closing his eyes. Taking a deep breath, he allowed the tension to dissipate from his body. He desperately needed a moment of peace. The silence enveloped him as he sat there, his fingers gripping the steering wheel so tightly his knuckles turned white. The gentle purr of the engine, now idle, and the hum of the AC became a faint backdrop to his thoughts.

Lord, help. I need guidance here. Direction. I don't even know what I need. You. I guess I need You.

A comforting peace quietly snaked through his soul. God was still with him. Even if Devon did not know what to do with his raging emotions, he was not alone. Perhaps, in time, he could forgive his parents for their lies.

Opening his eyes, he straightened his posture, a newfound determination etched across his face. The world outside beckoned, and he was ready to face it head-on. Taking one last moment to collect himself, he shifted the gear into Drive, propelling himself forward into the unknown, armed with newfound strength and resilience.

As he parked by the children's building, he hoped he could avoid seeing Mami or Papi for a while. He needed more time to… What? He did not know. Perhaps the mission trip in a few weeks would provide the break he needed, allowing him time to adjust.

When Devon entered his office, he noticed the slip of paper on his desk with a bright blue sticky note. *Mijo, please let us tell your brother in our time. Love, Mami.*

He snorted as he crumpled the sticky note and tossed it in the trash. Then he turned over the piece of paper to reveal his official birth certificate. A quick glance into the children's center assured him Raina had everything under control. So, he pivoted and headed out the door, grabbing his passport paperwork on the way.

If only he hadn't wanted to leave home—to go on the mission trip. Then he never would have known that his life had been a lie. That his birth parents died when he was too young to remember them. He clenched his fists tightly on the steering wheel as he drove away from the ranch, trying to suppress the pain that threatened to consume him.

"RAINA?"

She lifted her gaze away from the sweet Elena Vargas, glad to provide River a brief respite from the twins. With three care workers on duty, Raina devoted most of her attention to the twins that morning.

"Good morning, Catalina," she greeted the older woman. She noticed the sheen in the sweet woman's dark eyes before she looked away.

"Have you... Seen Devon?"

"Not for a few hours. He said he had some errands to run and might not be back for a while."

Catalina's gaze shifted to her grandchildren, and her expression softened. She closed the distance and rested a hand on Elena's head. A nostalgic look filled her eyes as if she relived long-forgotten memories.

"Has she been good today?"

Raina's heart warmed as happiness washed over her. "She's been quiet. Slept most of the day since River dropped her off."

"She reminds me of... The little girl we lost."

When a tear slid down Catalina's cheek, Raina grabbed a few tissues from a nearby shelf. Then she led her into Devon's office.

"Did you want to talk about it?" she offered as Catalina sat.

"We never spoke about her. Not for years, until Tres' papi told Derin about her last spring." Catalina's shoulders rose and fell with her deep sigh. "So many secrets we've kept. We thought we were doing the right thing. Protecting them..."

Raina shifted Elena to her other arm, relishing the warmth of the little girl nestled against her chest. Elena nuzzled her face against her neck. Oh, how she wanted a baby of her own. Even if someone could love her, as unlikely as it seemed, it would never happen once they learned her secret. She locked the thought away. Right now, Catalina clearly needed a listening ear.

"What happened?"

Catalina angled to face her, sorrow crinkling the corners of her eyes. "She passed away as a toddler. We had told none of the boys about her. Tres and I thought it would be easier for them if they didn't know about their... Losses."

When Catalina stood, she straightened her shoulders and lifted her chin. She withdrew a piece of paper from her purse. Then she snagged a post-it note and pen before jotting down something. After leaving the paper on Devon's desk, she turned.

"Thank you for listening."

She smiled at Raina and her granddaughter before she turned and breezed back into the main room. Braden's gleeful greeting echoed before Catalina's response faded.

Raina stood and gently laid the sleeping infant in the crib before she picked up a mewling Sloane. The odor wafting from him let her know the reason for his complaints. She grabbed a clean diaper from the bag River had left before she changed him.

When she returned to the main room, she glimpsed Devon. The tense set of his jaw and scowl on his face kept her from checking on him. A moment later, he stormed out through the door to the resort office. She released a soft breath.

He hadn't been the same for over a week. The fun, inquisitive cowboy had withdrawn. From his family, the children, and her.

Raina scolded herself. He was her boss, nothing more.

Not her friend. Other than casual coworker conversation, she knew little about him and he knew just as little about her.

Since that almost kiss at his family's home—was it almost two weeks ago now—she kept her distance. All conversation remained professional, what little there had been. Josh, Amber, and Taylor answered more of her questions than Devon had.

Still, Raina needed to press him for time to learn his responsibilities before he left on his mission trip in a few weeks. She needed to learn the computer system, and whatever else he busied himself with in his office for hours on end.

"Raina?" Braden called for her as she settled Sloane in the crib.

"Yes?"

"Can you walk with me over to the stables? Dad said I could hang out with him if I got bored."

Raina scanned the room. Matt's mom had picked him up a half hour ago. None of the other kids were near Braden's age.

"You feel up to the walk in the heat? Or should I drive you over?"

"Do you have a booster seat?"

Raina shook her head, realizing she shouldn't drive him without it.

"Maybe we can borrow Rennie's golf cart. Scout lays down on the floor, and I hold on real tight."

Raina smiled. "Golf cart sounds perfect. I'll go get the keys."

She entered the resort office and Solana grabbed a key ring for her.

"If I'm at lunch, you can leave the key on my desk."

"Thanks!"

Raina drove the cart next to the children's entrance. Josh held the door open for Braden and Scout. Braden grasped the harness on Scout's back, using her for balance as he walked on his blades to the golf cart. Then he climbed onto the seat next to her. Raina waited for the dog to lie down in the back before she drove the cart over to the stable.

"Uncle Dev is sad a lot."

The little boy's observation surprised her. "Why do you say that?"

"He used to play with us more. And he missed family dinner on Sunday. I miss him."

Raina's heart squeezed tight. "He told you about his trip?"

"Yeah, he's going to teach kids far away about Jesus."

"I think he's been busy getting ready for that trip."

"I will miss him when he's gone."

Raina eased the golf cart near the stable entrance. Then she stood, ready to help Braden down from the cart. He didn't need it. Scout jumped down first. Then Braden used the big dog's back to steady himself as he stepped down. He held onto the harness and walked toward the stable. She held the door open for him and the dog before following him to Dylan's office.

"Dad!"

"Hey, Braden." Dylan Vargas looked up. "Come to keep me company?"

"Yeah. Can I groom my pony?"

"Soon. I need to finish up on the computer, then we can go see your pony."

Raina smiled as Dylan approached her.

"Everything okay?"

"Yeah. Matt's mom picked him up so Braden was a little bored."

Dylan chuckled. "Thanks for bringing him by."

"No problem."

As she started to turn away, he asked, "Is Devon okay?"

Raina paused in the doorway, surprised he thought she would know. "I think so. Why do you ask?"

Dylan's eyes darted to his son before they met her gaze. "He's made himself scarce. From me. The family."

She shrugged, uncertain what to add.

"Thanks for bringing Braden over. You have my number? I can pick him up if he asks again."

Raina added his contact to her phone and headed back out to the cart. Right as she climbed onto the golf cart, Devon pulled up next to her. He hopped out of his truck. Frowning and looking down at the ground, he headed toward the stables.

"Hey, Devon!" she called after him.

He whirled around before walking toward her. She met him halfway.

"I've been meaning to talk to you," she said.

"I'm sorry. I know I still have a lot to go over with you. And to clean out the office."

It surprised her he would move out of his office. Though it shouldn't. After all, she was there to replace him.

"No rush." Raina's arms suddenly seemed in the way, so she propped her hands in her back pockets as she looked up into his gorgeous eyes. Sadness reflected in their depths before he masked it.

"I'm running out of time. Only two more weeks before I head off to Guatemala."

"I'm sure we'll get through everything."

Devon lifted his cowboy hat, running a hand through his hair. "I'm sorry I've been so…"

"Distracted?"

Red covered his neck and face. "Yeah."

The silence stretched for several seconds, leaving Raina feeling awkward. She scuffed her combat boot in the dust.

"You know how to ride horses, right?" she ventured.

"Of course."

"It's probably too much to ask."

"What?"

"Do you think you could teach me? I mean, if you're too

busy, Renata and Solana said they could—"

"I'll do it. I was just going to go for a ride, so we can saddle up some horses and ride in the arena instead."

Excitement bubbled in her chest. "I'd like that. Let me take the golf cart back."

"Yeah. Okay. Meet me at the arena."

Raina flashed him a grin before darting to the golf cart, surprised by how much she looked forward to the lesson. Or spending time with the troubled cowboy.

7

———————

DEVON DID NOT know what possessed him to agree to Raina's request to teach her how to ride horses. Something about her drew him in. He wanted to spend more time with her. Perhaps distancing himself from his family didn't mean he had to distance from her too.

He entered the stable and led Athena, his lovely chestnut quarter horse, to the grooming area. Braden and Dylan appeared a minute later.

"Dev, it's good to see you."

"Dyl."

"Going for a ride?"

"Gonna teach Raina how to ride. At the arena."

"Let me pick a horse for her," Dylan said before clasping Braden's free hand.

Father and son walked down the alleyway to Braden's pony's stall. The sight pulled on his heartstrings. Had his father lived, would he have taught Devon how to care for his horse? Or taught him how to ride? Would he have enjoyed time outdoors or preferred working in an office? Would he have come back from the war as the same man who left?

Devon pounded his chest with a fisted hand, trying to jar the emptiness loose. He knew nothing about his father. Did he have green eyes like Devon? Or dark brown eyes like Drake? Did Devon favor him or his mother? Would she have read him bed-time stories, tucking him in with a soft lullaby?

He tried to reach deep into his memories but always came up blank.

Turning his attention to Athena, Devon groomed his mare. With each stroke of the currycomb, he tried to force the gloomy thoughts aside. He did not want to bring Raina down with his foul mood.

"I brought Caramel for Raina."

At the sound of Dylan's voice, Devon looked up. "Thanks."

"I'll groom her so you don't keep Raina waiting."

"Where's Braden?"

"He's talking to his pony."

Devon nodded.

"So… You missed family dinner."

Devon rounded to the other side of Athena where Dylan couldn't see him, rolling his eyes.

"I take it you talked to Mami and Papi? Didn't like what they said?"

"Yes. It… I was right. They aren't my parents. Or Drake's."

"Does Drake know?"

"No. And Mami asked me to let them tell him in their time."

"I'm sorry, Dev. I know this must be h-h-hard."

Devon let out a long breath, reining in his emotions. Athena's ears flicked, warning him he was doing a terrible job of it. He appreciated Dylan's empathy—obvious from his brief stutter.

"For what it's worth, I plan to still call you brother. We always have been and always will be."

Dylan smoothed out the saddle pad on Caramel's back before slinging the saddle onto it. Then he shortened the stirrups to match Raina's stature. Devon could adjust them to the perfect length when he helped Raina up at the arena. Heat warmed his face.

"I appreciate it, Dyl."

Thinking of him as a cousin didn't seem right. They were brothers. Even if they once hadn't been. What had Papi said? That's right. They adopted Devon and Drake as their own. Guess that made his brothers officially brothers instead of cousins.

Devon finished saddling Athena before thanking Dylan for his help. Then he led the horses out of the stables before mounting Athena. He rode at a walk over to the nearby arena. They used a swamp cooler at the arena most days, taking the edge off the worst of the afternoon heat. An air conditioner, which was more expensive to run, removed the moisture from the air. They reserved its use for the hottest monsoon months when it worked better than the swamp cooler.

Why these random facts came to mind, Devon did not know. His mind had always latched on to facts, dates, and geography. Probably why history appealed to him so much. It was a useful skill in school, helping him achieve straight A's throughout high school and college. Mami called him bright.

He dismounted Athena and tied both horses by the arena ring. The narrow windows at the top of the arena walls allowed a stream of natural light to filter in, casting a soft glow in the space as Devon made his way to the control room to turn on the lights. He waved to Raina as he walked back to the horses.

"Ever been around horses?" he asked, stopping next to her.

"Never." A grin spread across her face, brightening the entire place. "But I've always wanted to."

"A few things before we approach the horses. They are animals with minds of their own. They can react to strong emotions, whether positive or negative. So it's important to be calm and in control when working with horses."

Raina schooled her features, though a corner of her

mouth twitched, causing Devon's to quirk up for a second. Adorable.

Before he realized what he was doing, he clasped her hand loosely and led her toward the horses. A spark passed between them, shifting his heart rate a little higher. He stopped by Caramel.

"This is Caramel. She's very gentle. Great with new riders. Dylan suggested her for you. We'll take a few minutes for you two to meet."

Raina lifted her hand, ready to touch Caramel's white blaze. She bit her lip and raised an eyebrow, uncertainty written all over her face. "Like this?"

Devon nodded right before Raina's hand rested lightly on the horse.

"Oh!" Her eyes went wide. "She's so soft."

He smiled, enchanted by her delight. So pure and sweet. Again, the silent siren song wove around his heart, beckoning him closer to her. He cleared his throat and stepped back, before handing her an apple slice.

"She loves apples. Place it in your palm and hold your hand out. Like this."

Devon demonstrated with Athena, and his horse gummed his hand, gently gobbling up the treat.

Raina held her palm toward Caramel. The mare tenderly accepted the apple slice from Raina's hand. A giggle escaped for a second before she sucked the sides of her mouth together, making fish-lips in her attempt to control her emotions.

Devon laughed.

"That was amazing! What's next?"

Devon gave a few more tips before he suggested she sit on Caramel's back.

"How do I get up there?"

This woman. Everything about her sent his senses on high alert. He loved her child-like reverence of the horse and the process.

"Normally, there's a mounting block around some-where." His eyes scanned the area. Not finding it, he planned to give her a leg up. He cupped his hands together.

"Place the ball of your foot in my hands and bounce up. I'll provide the extra momentum as you swing your other leg over the horse."

He crouched a little to make it easier for her. When she placed her hands on his shoulders, his breath caught. The sweet scent—something like honey and peaches—floated up from her hair as it accidentally brushed against his cheek. Devon summoned all his self control not to wrap his arms around her. Their eyes connected, and he saw the dreamy look in her gaze before she stammered.

"Uh. Like this?"

At last, her combat boot rested on his interlocked fingers. She pushed up as he guided her higher and onto Caramel's back. Her melodic giggles echoed in the empty arena.

She fake whispered with rounded eyes, "I'm. Sitting. On. A. Horse."

Those amazing green eyes sparkled with abandon. Devon stared. He couldn't help it. He had seen no one more beautiful than Raina at that moment. An awkward number of seconds passed before he tore his eyes away from her, heat warming his entire face. At least his hat shaded his embarrassment from her view. He hoped.

He shortened the stirrups another notch before he showed her the proper way to rest her foot in them. Then he explained how to make Caramel move forward. When Raina seemed to have the hang of it, Devon mounted Athena and rode next to her.

"How do I make her change directions?"

A chuckle burst from him. Then he laid his reins across Athena's neck, showing her. Raina did the same, a titter floating on the air.

"She's so smart."

Devon smiled. "She's well-trained. And calm. Used to

lots of different riders."

"And smart." Raina teased.

"And smart."

The rest of the afternoon flew by as Devon taught Raina the basics. The heaviness of the past few weeks lightened as he shared in her joyfulness. She was good for him. Helped him forget his pain. In the far reaches of his subconscious, he almost admitted it would be hard to leave her.

RAINA COULD HARDLY contain her excitement as they rode the horses back toward the stable. She learned how to ride a horse! A huge animal! And it was so much fun.

Even better, Devon finally relaxed, and she felt like she saw the real man. He broke down all the steps in a way she understood. He would be a phenomenal teacher. She would miss this version of him when he left for the mission trip. She wondered if he would spend much time at the ranch before he started teaching in the fall.

"Have you lined up a teaching job yet?"

Devon's smile faded, and she wished she hadn't asked.

"I've applied to a few school districts on the west side of Phoenix. I also let the Wickenburg High School principal know. He said they didn't have any openings. If nothing else, I can substitute teach until something permanent opens up."

"Isn't Phoenix far from here?"

"An hour or so."

Raina's shoulders dropped, and her joy dimmed. He would move away.

"I'll get an apartment near whatever school I end up at."

"Oh."

She had hoped he would stick around the ranch. Perhaps he would visit on Sundays for family meals, not that she had been invited back for those. Except Braden said he already scaled back his involvement with his family. The thought made her dejected.

"You want to grab a sandwich in town?"

The question surprised her. When it finally registered, she agreed. "I'd love to." Anything to get to know Devon Vargas better. If nothing else, she could be his friend. A listening ear for the heartache of his life.

She had never had a friend before.

When they led the horses to the grooming area, two cowboys volunteered to take care of them. Devon thanked them and led her back out to his 4Runner.

"You want to drop your car by your place first?"

"Sure."

"Great. I'll meet you over there."

As Raina sat in her car, all she could smell was horse. She asked Devon to give her time to change. Twenty minutes later, she climbed into his vehicle as he held the door.

"I haven't been off the ranch other than to pick up a few groceries or household items," she admitted as he backed out of the spot.

"Let's drive around town, then. I'll show you where everything is and we can go to the steakhouse instead."

Devon's kindness touched her deeply. She sniffed and squeaked out her agreement.

Raina watched as the desert plants whizzed by once he merged onto the highway. Mountains provided a stunning view along three horizons. Tall saguaro cacti dotted the landscape along with scrub brush and palo verde trees. Renata explained to her last weekend the names of most of the desert plants.

"The desert is so beautiful," she whispered.

"Yeah. Most tourists think it's all brown and dirt."

"How long do the white flowers stay on the saguaro?"

Devon held the steering wheel with one hand and rested

his forearm on the console between them. It would have been so easy to take his hand and lace her fingers with his. The thought startled Raina enough that she clasped her hands together in her lap. He was her employer. She couldn't think of this as a date. It was just two acquaintances becoming friends.

"Less than twenty-four hours."

"What?" She angled to look at him. His face was completely serious.

"They open overnight and native bats actually pollinate them. So do bees and other long-beaked birds. Then they die by the next evening."

"But there are so many blooms."

"Yeah. But each individual one's lifespan is a day. They turn into fruit that grows through mid-to-late-June."

"Huh. Who knew? Oh, I guess you did. Smarty pants."

Devon laughed. "My brothers..." A frown replaced his smile before he continued. "They hated playing trivia games with me. I remember the weirdest stuff."

"A trait which will come in handy in the classroom, I'm sure."

For the rest of the drive to town, he shared other facts about the desert plants. Raina enjoyed listening to him. He came across as knowledgeable but not offputting, like some guys in college.

When they neared the town, he showed her the big grocery store with better prices than the one she had been shopping at. He also drove past a shopping center with western clothes, a local café, and other stores. Then he drove her to the old downtown area. He parked, and they walked along the sidewalk in front of the quaint places.

"This is where all the tourists shop. During holiday weekends, we usually have events from September through April. Things like parades, Wild West shootout shows, stagecoach rides, and more."

"I'll have to see if my boss will let me have a day off in

September to check it out."

A shadow fell over his face. "You'll be the boss."

"Oh. I guess I will." Sadness wrapped around her, but she forced it away. She would enjoy the evening with Devon. Even if he would leave her soon, too.

He cleared his throat. "Hungry?"

"Starving. I think I missed lunch."

His warm hand closed around hers. She wondered if he even realized he held her hand. She couldn't help but notice, as his touch sent her heart and mind racing. Longing for a future full of companionship filled the lonely hole in her chest. Friends didn't hold hands.

When they stopped at the passenger side of his vehicle, he finally released her hand, opening the door for her. In that moment, she felt more treasured than ever before. This smart cowboy rattled her—made her want something more.

Raina stared up into his handsome face. His face softened as his eyes searched hers. She moistened her suddenly dry lips, breath stuck in her throat when he swayed forward slightly. As if he realized he moved, he jolted back, running a hand over the back of his neck.

Then he winked at her. "Should I give you a leg up?"

A snort exploded from her. "I'm not *that* short."

Once she slid into the seat, he closed the door. Raina let out a soft puff of air. Surely, he noticed the connection between them.

8

———

DEVON SLOWLY WALKED around his truck, trying to calm his speeding pulse. Raina turned him inside out whenever they shared space together.

He had almost kissed her again. He shouldn't do that. Couldn't do that. Falling for her wouldn't be fair to her. Or him. She worked for his family — for him. But he was leaving the ranch soon. Had no intention of coming back for long once he returned from the mission trip.

So why was he taking her to the steakhouse? A date place? It wasn't a date.

If he were as smart as his mami claimed he was, he would head to a place with a drive thru and drop her at her home. The steakhouse felt too much like a date. Especially given the cute pink floral strappy, sun dress she threw on with those wedge sandals.

Devon groaned and took a steadying breath before he opened the driver's side door and hopped into his 4Runner. The engine revved as he turned the AC full blast. He made the mistake of glancing at Raina to see the breeze blow those gorgeous curls away from her neck. Did she have any idea how attractive she looked?

She flashed him a sweet smile before he stirred himself from his thoughts. Then he backed out of the spot and drove to the steakhouse in silence.

Once settled at their table, Raina started the conversation.

"The other day when you... You know..."

Devon expelled a rough breath. "Made a mess of the office?"

"Yeah." She took a sip of water before continuing. "Do you want to talk about it?"

"Sorry, I've been so weird. Tense."

He waited for the server to place their salads on the table.

"I just found out that the people I thought were my parents weren't. They are really my aunt and uncle."

When Raina choked on a bite of her salad, Devon leaned forward in his seat, ready to Heimlich her if needed. She pounded her dainty hand against her chest a few times before drinking a gulp of water.

"You okay?"

"Yeah. So your aunt and uncle?"

"I've been bugging Mami about my birth certificate for a long time. Needed it to finish my passport application."

"For the mission trip?"

"Right. When I finally saw it, I discovered my parents' names were Devon, Sr. and Anita."

"Oh! Not Catalina or Tres—er, whatever his name is."

Devon stuffed a forkful of salad in his mouth as he nodded.

"What happened?"

For only a minute, he debated whether to share the heartbreaking details. After a stern warning not to share anything with Drake, he unburdened his soul. He appreciated Raina's occasional question. Their entrées arrived right as he finished the tale.

"So I guess you could say I'm an orphan," Devon finished.

His heart stabbed when she dropped her hands into her lap and looked down at them. Her entire demeanor shifted. Then he remembered. She had been an orphan.

"At least you had someone who loved you."

Devon's stomach squeezed tight, killing his appetite. Here he had been complaining about his family's secrets, instead of seeing the blessing of his aunt and uncle raising him as a son. Guilt coiled around him. He might be far from ready to forgive them for lying all these years, but he could not fault them for how well they cared for him and Drake.

He reached across the table, resting his hand palm up. Then he wiggled his fingers. A few heartbeats thudded in his chest before she placed her delicate hand in his. He rubbed his thumb over her smooth skin.

"I'm sorry. I must sound completely ungrateful to you."

Raina's gaze finally wandered to his. He saw the pain there.

"I know the secret hurt you," she said. "But they loved you, right? You didn't live in fear of being abandoned again or... Worse."

Devon slid his hand back to his side of the table. "Yes, they loved me. Still do. Adopted both me and Drake."

She nodded slowly before cutting off a piece of chicken. She pushed it around on her plate, not making eye contact with him again.

What a jerk he must appear to her. How could he fix this?

"Raina, do you want to tell me about it? Your past?"

Her eyelids fluttered downward, hiding those green windows to her soul for a moment. Then they appeared again, looking far away.

"After my parents, I entered the foster system. They shuffled me from home to home. Most of the time, I did not know if I would be safe. Some of the group home workers or foster parents were mean. Abusive. I learned to be quiet. Do what I was told. Stay off their radar."

"I thought... Sometimes still do... That I am not worthy of love. That I'm,..." She coughed, and a tear slid down her rosy cheek. His heart ached for her. "Trash."

Devon set his silverware down. Then he stood and rounded the table. He held out his hands and tugged her to her feet before folding her close to his chest. She clutched fistfuls of the back of his shirt as her tears soaked the front.

When the server came by, he reached into his back pocket with one hand and retrieved his card. The server understood his intent and brought back boxes for the food, along with the receipt.

"Raina, sweetheart, we can go."

A muffled sniffle sounded as she eased away from him.

"I'm so sorry I ruined the meal."

Devon kept his arm around her as he kissed the top of her head. That sweet honey and peaches fragrance smelled comforting.

"We'll take it home for later."

He released her and slid his card in his wallet before snatching up the bag with their to-go boxes. Then he rested his arm around her back, lightly placing his hand on her waist.

"Come on. I'll take you home."

She nodded against his side as she clutched his waist with one arm.

Devon pried Raina from him as he helped her into his truck. Then he circled it, dropping the boxed dinner on the back seat before climbing behind the wheel.

His stomach ached, not even slightly tempted by the delicious aroma now filling the enclosed space. Why was he always making this sweet woman cry?

"I'm. S-s-sorry." Her voice quavered between sobs.

He reached across the console and held her hand as he drove back to the ranch.

"I don't mean. To fall. Apart. At every. Meal."

"Raina, it's fine."

From his peripheral he caught her staring at him. He glanced over to see her slumped shoulders.

"It's not fine. Some day I will get over my —" Her voice

cracked. "Past."

Devon became keenly aware of her pain, feeling it nearly as deeply as she did. He could not imagine the utter loneliness and fear she grew up with. What kind of jerk was he that he took his aunt and uncle's act of love for granted? They adopted him as their own. Treated him as a son. They had given him everything he needed and more.

And here, the kind Raina had felt discarded. No one had cared for her. No one adopted her. She clearly grew up in the school of hard knocks.

He rubbed his thumb over her knuckles. The sound of tires whirred against the highway pavement. The AC fan blew softly in the background, accompanying her stuttered snuffles.

Lord, help me be a comfort to Raina. Show me what to say or do.

RAINA COULD SCARCELY believe she broke down at dinner. Clutching Devon like a lifeline. Soaking his shirt with her tears. Could she not make it through one meal with this man without dissolving into hysterics? Surely, by now, he regretted ever meeting her. Would probably doubt her ability to do her job.

"Raina. It's okay to feel what you're feeling."

The warmth of his hand covering hers helped soothe her aching heart. How many days had she longed for the tender touch of another human being? A hug. A pat on the hand. Anything.

Sometimes she wondered if it would have been easier growing up in the system from birth instead of having known the love of parents, only to have it ripped away. Every day growing up, she recalled just how much she had lost. Love. Care. Safety. Peace. Things she hadn't truly felt, besides those few months at the Radcliff's, until she aged out and started college. Even then, she missed feeling loved and accepted.

"I… Life after my parents passed has been very hard."

Devon's thumb swiped back and forth over her knuckles. She savored his tenderness.

"I hadn't realized how much until I came here. Saw your parents. How much they care for every person in their family, whether their own children, nieces and nephews, grandchildren, daughters-in-law."

"I'm sorry." Raina heard the heaviness in his voice.

"It's not your fault." She snorted. "It's no one's fault. It just was. Is."

After Devon cleared his throat, he spoke. "You are a wonderful person, Raina. The way you love the kids at the center. You give them attention. Treat them like each one is special."

He removed his hand as they turned onto the dirt road back to the ranch. Gravel crunched under the weight of the tires. The sun lowered closer to the horizon, casting long shadows across the desert landscape. The reddish tones of Dalton Peak turned a deep rust outlined in dark purple hues.

She didn't complain when he drove toward a private road instead of taking her straight home. She wasn't ready to face her roommates' questions.

When Devon parked in front of the gate, he left his vehicle running and got out to open the gate. Then he drove for several minutes until he parked on a ledge overlooking the massive valley below. The light tan of the desert floor turned a dark brown as the white flowers of the saguaro tinged gold in the fading rays of the sun.

Though he angled toward her, she kept her gaze on the setting sun. The beautiful scene helped her angst ease, allowing the peace of God to fill her soul again.

When Raina turned to Devon, his eyes filled with a mix

of curiosity and apprehension. There was an unspoken understanding between them, a connection that went beyond mere words.

Devon broke the silence, his voice filled with a hint of vulnerability. "I wanted to show you something," he whispered, his gaze fixed on the vast expanse before them. "This place... it's special to me."

She nodded, her heart pounding with anticipation. It was in moments like these, away from prying eyes and judgment, that she could truly be herself. She could let her guard down and simply exist.

As the last rays of sunlight danced across the valley, casting an ethereal glow, she couldn't help but feel a sense of awe. It was as if the landscape mirrored her journey — the rugged terrain representing the challenges she had faced, and the golden hues signifying the warmth blossoming in her heart for this man.

The first stars flickered in the sky, and her gaze slipped toward Devon. His eyes glistened before they darted away.

"You must think I'm a shallow fool."

Lost in the moment's beauty, she reached out and took his hand in hers. She intertwined her fingers with his, silently reassuring him he was not alone. The fading light painted his face with a soft glow, emphasizing their deepening connection.

"Devon, there is no benefit in comparing our pain. Yours is just as valid as mine, though grown out of different roots. If either of us is in the wrong, it's me for being jealous — for coveting what you have."

"No. It's normal to want a loving family. There's no jealousy in wanting what should be a normal life."

Raina scoffed. "Look at us. More concerned about comforting the other's pain than dealing with our own."

Devon's mouth quirked in a half-smile. "You are an amazing woman. That's why I have no doubts that you will be the best children's director this place has ever seen. Your heart is gigantic, with an unending supply of love. No one would ever guess you grew up without it."

She closed her eyes and rested her head against the seat back.

"Jesus has worked on me. I used to be bitter. Now, I try not to think about the past. He rescued me so that—"

She stopped abruptly, not ready to share her dream with him. She couldn't be sure he would trust her with the ranch's children's center if he thought she might leave one day.

"So that?"

Raina shook her head. "It doesn't matter."

He reached over and laced his fingers with hers. "So you don't think I'm a jerk?"

"No!" She shook her head, punctuating the word. "You have an enormous heart, too. Planning a mission trip to Guatemala. To work with kids?"

"Yeah. My friend Greg started working at a non-profit a few years ago. He went on a trip down there and came back so on fire for God. He told me stories about the poverty there. How hungry and thirsty the little kids are to learn about Jesus. They had to cancel the trip last year, due to funding issues. So I've been planning this trip for almost two years."

"Wow. When do you leave?"

"Two weeks."

"Nervous?"

"Yeah."

"I'll pray for you."

Just then, his stomach growled, and she recalled their uneaten meal.

"I don't suppose they gave us plastic ware with our food?" she asked.

Devon released her hand and stretched his arm to grab their boxes. He opened the bag and popped the lid on the first container before handing it to her. Then he opened his.

The delicious aroma of grilled chicken and steak filled the cab.

"Nope. No plastic ware."

Raina picked up her chicken breast with her fingers and bit off a chunk with gusto.

Devon's laughter filled the space. "Guess our meal is now finger food."

"Yeah. For some reason, I'm starving!" She giggled before taking another bite.

Raina relaxed as he gnawed on a mouthful of his steak. They ate together in silence, watching the stars dot the night sky. Despite her tumultuous emotions earlier, she couldn't recall a better afternoon or evening in her life. The horseback riding session. The tour around town. Then him treating her to a fine meal, even if they delayed eating it. His caring attention and comforting words. Just his presence eased some of her pain.

When they finished the meal, Devon dug through the cubby in the console between them, producing a stack of napkins. They both wiped their hands before he placed the trash in the bag, dropping it behind their seats.

"Thanks for a great evening, Raina."

Her heart levitated within her. "I should thank you."

Devon backed his vehicle from the spot. "You do not know how much I needed this. Thinking about something other than my family secret. It's weighed me down since I learned of it."

After he hopped out to lock the gate, he rested his arm on the console and she threaded her fingers with his, savoring the warmth of his touch.

"I'm glad talking to me helped."

His strong hand tightened around hers. "You gave me a fresh perspective. It means a lot."

When he parked in front of the women's housing, he climbed out of his vehicle and rounded it, opening the door for her. She placed her dainty hand into his as she slid from the seat. My, he was so tall. He reached down, placing his hand on her cheek. The gentle touch sent waves of longing through her. Such a simple connection. Yet, she wanted to memorize the moment. Save it as a hope of what her life could one day become. He leaned down, and she closed her eyes in anticipation.

The expected kiss never came. At the last second, he wrapped his powerful arms around her. She leaned into his muscular abdomen before sliding her arms around his waist. She lost count of the seconds they embraced before he leaned back.

"Thanks again, Raina. I'll clear out the office tomorrow and show you the computer system."

The mention of work snapped her out of her blissful dreaming. If she wasn't careful, she might fall for the handsome, godly cowboy. And she didn't think it was a good idea. He was her employer. Besides, he had ambitions that would take him away from there—from her, leaving her heartbroken again. No, she must stop her heart from drawing closer to him. Starting tomorrow morning, she would put some distance between them. Keep things on a friend level. She could do that, right?

As she walked toward her home, Raina couldn't keep from one last glimpse over her shoulder. Devon smiled and gave a little wave, warming her from head to toe as she ducked inside.

9

———————

DEVON'S HEART FELT full in the most pleasing way. As dates went, it could have been a disaster. Yet, leaving the restaurant and driving toward his favorite sunset lookout salvaged it.

Though he really should not think about it as a date. He had no intention of falling in love. He had a mission trip to go on. A new job to find and start. None of those things left room for a serious relationship.

Still, Raina had felt perfect in his arms. Her kindness knew no bounds. She had not judged him for his hurt about his family secret revealed and the betrayal he felt from it. Instead, she reacted with understanding and compassion.

Who did that?

A godly woman. The kind of woman he wanted as a life partner. Someone who would stick with him forever.

Ugh. He should not think about her as wife material. He was her employer. He had plans. Plans that didn't leave space for a family of his own. Not now. Maybe in a few years.

Would she wait a few years? Would she need time, too?

Devon cut the engine and dropped his head back against the headrest of his seat. Where had these thoughts come from?

One amazing afternoon with Raina and her siren song ensnared him—without her even trying. Is this what falling in love felt like?

He kind of wished he could ask Dylan. Except Dylan had loved Brisa for a good decade before she noticed him. Derin? Yeah, no. Would it be dumb to talk to his romance writer sister-in-law, River?

Devon eased his door open and hung his long legs over the side until his feet connected with dirt. Standing to his full height, he inhaled the sweet night air. He had always been better at helping others sort through their feelings than sorting through his own.

When he nudged the door to the bunkhouse open, the TV echoed down the hall. He turned left toward his bunk. Years ago, the room held private bunks for the Vargas sons. After Derin moved out, they opened up the space to others. Adan reclined on his bunk, long legs stretched out, crossed at the ankles. He looked up from a book, nodding his head in acknowledgement.

"Hey," Devon greeted.

Drake entered the room, towel wrapped around his waist, damp hair flopped over his brow. "You were out late."

Devon shrugged.

"Hot date?" Adan teased, marking his place in his book before snapping it shut.

Devon's face and neck burned.

"Really?" Drake asked. "With who?"

"Raina."

"Wow. Does she know you plan to leave?"

Devon toed off his boots and dropped his hat on a hook by his bunk. Guilt pinched his gut, knowing he had to keep her in the friend zone. It'd break her heart to let her think there could be a future with him. At least not now.

"Yeah," he answered at length.

The lights across the hall flipped off. Ross Braxton, the newest member of their bunk area, entered. His dark eyes darted around the room. "Did I miss something?"

"Naw. Just Devon going on a date," Drake teased.

Devon held back a groan. Thankfully, Ross only nodded. He was so new he didn't understand the significance of Devon going on a date. He checked the thermostat and climbed into his bed without further interaction.

Drake, much to Devon's annoyance, sat down on the corner of Devon's bunk.

"Is she what's had you all tied up in knots the last couple of weeks?"

Devon started to shake his head before he caught himself. He couldn't tell Drake about their parents. First, because Mami asked him not to. Second, because Drake had an extremely close relationship with Catalina — the only mother he had ever known. Devon knew if the truth came out, it would wreck Drake. He couldn't be the one to do it.

Drake's dark eyes held his for several seconds. "Well, whatever it is, you know you can talk to me, right?"

Devon clasped his only true brother's shoulder, schooling his face. "I know."

Drake sat there for a few more seconds after Devon dropped his hand to his lap. Then his younger brother stood and donned a pair of boxers before laying down on his bunk.

Devon crossed the room and flipped off the main switch before readying himself for bed.

Yeah, it was going to tear up Drake to learn the truth. Hopefully, God would surround him with people to talk to when it did, just like He had brought Raina for him.

THE NEXT MORNING, Raina woke to the sound of her alarm on her phone. The cheery chirping birds brought a smile to her face as she threw back the covers. What a glorious day!

Memories of Devon from the previous day kept her smile in place while warming her insides in the most delightful way. She still wasn't sure she wanted to be only friends, but she needed to try. Besides, it didn't mean she couldn't enjoy his company, right?

She donned a pair of jeans, a bright yellow t-shirt, and her trusty combat boots before heading over to the dining hall for breakfast. Drake greeted her with a knowing smile, causing her to wonder if Devon had said something about her. She shrugged it off while she ordered a hot latte with a dash of caramel and one of the to-go breakfast sandwiches from the coffee bar. With her employee discount, the price didn't break the bank, especially now that she had a steady income. She deserved a little treat.

When Drake set her items on the bar, Raina snagged them and darted toward the door, running headlong into a tall cowboy. Warm hands curled around her arms, steadying her.

"Whoa, there."

Raina's eyes traveled up Devon's shirt, disappointed to see a wet spot spreading over it. At least it had been a dark color. Maybe her coffee wouldn't leave a permanent stain.

"I'm so sorry."

"Not to worry, I'll grab a fresh one."

As he pulled the hot coffee splotch away from him, Raina's cheeks flushed. It had to burn his skin, especially since he wiggled it to keep it from settling against his oh-so-perfect torso. She had to stop thinking like that.

He flashed her a smile before he held the door open for her.

"See you in a few minutes."

She ducked her head and hurried inside the children's center, grateful he had already unlocked the doors. Amber and Taylor greeted her on her way to the break room. She slid a chair away from the small table with her foot as she set her coffee and sandwich down. After peeking under the lid of her coffee, relief washed over her. At least she hadn't dumped too much of it on Devon.

Raina offered a quick prayer before eating her breakfast sandwich. Then she sipped her latte until she heard the front door open. She peered around the entry of the breakroom, relieved to see Devon's fresh shirt hadn't dampened his spirits.

"I thought we could go over several things on the computer today."

She offered a tentative smile before she followed him into the office. Blinking, she realized he had cleared away all his personal things. A few rows of almost empty bookshelves ran along the windows. The scent of lemon wood polish lingered in the air.

"I left a few resource books we bought for the center."

"Thanks."

She ran a hand over the beautiful woodgrain on the top of the bookshelves, wondering what she might put there. Raina owned very few personal possessions. She thought she might have a framed picture of her parents hidden in the box she never opened. Then she thought better of it. Too much pain to look at the picture daily.

"If you want a different desk or chair, just let Rennie know. She'll order it."

Raina nodded before Devon stepped out of the room for a minute. Then he wheeled a second office chair over to the desk. He patted it. "Take a seat."

As she sat, she caught the pine and cedar scent from him, breathing a little deeper to enjoy it. Heat warmed her cheeks. She really should not keep thinking about Devon Vargas like this, not if she expected to remain just friends.

He punched the power button on the computer and slid the keyboard and mouse in front of her.

"Here's your login info. You should change your password after the first login to something you can remember."

"I will." She quickly keyed in the info and the computer

screen flashed to a familiar generic blue with the manufacturer's logo.

Devon spent the next hour teaching her about the special software for managing the children's center. He had previously shown her the check-in part.

"You can take notes on the different kids. Here's where we mark allergies and the like. This right here is where we indicate if the child is a resort guest, a permanent worker's child, or a seasonal worker's child. For the permanent and seasonal workers, we subsidize some of the cost."

Raina made notes in her notepad. "Is there a way to email the chef the food allergies automatically based on what kids have checked in? That way, we don't have to do it manually?"

Devon rubbed a hand over his chin. "I never thought of doing that. If you can figure it out, I'm sure the chef would appreciate it."

After a few hours, Devon stood and stretched.

"Do you need help to bring over any personal items for your office?"

Raina's eyes darted to the floor. "I have nothing."

"Not even some books from college?"

"Only a few and I can manage those."

Devon's slight frown gave her pause. Perhaps he doubted her ability to run the place after all.

"If you need anything, please ask Rennie. We have a budget for resource materials and ongoing training for you and the staff."

"I will."

Devon wheeled the extra office chair toward the door to the resort office. He hesitated for a moment.

"About last night—"

"I know. We're just friends."

When a shadow passed over his face, Raina regretted her interruption.

"I was just going to say thanks for listening. And for

sharing about yourself."

"Yeah. Thanks to you, too."

A small smile turned up the corner of his mouth before he turned and wheeled the extra chair out of the room.

"Way to go, Raina," she muttered to herself, sliding the notebook to the corner of her desk.

She studied the room. It was her office now. She could work at the modern desk. And she would wait awhile before asking the Vargases for more books or supplies other than everyday things. With her formative years, she learned how to be content with what she had been given. One could not be disappointed if one did not long for more.

Yet, she did long for more. A man to love her for who she was. Children of her own—something she would never have, no matter how much she prayed for it.

Releasing a long breath, Raina sank against the office chair back. Her neck bent forward, a sign that the chair belonged to a much taller person. Maybe she would ask for a chair that fit her proportions better. She could always set Devon's chair in the corner. Keep it for him when he returned.

Except he wouldn't be working with her. He had other dreams, and that thought made her sad.

10

"YOU READY, BRO?"

Greg's voice came across the speakers of Devon's 4Runner while he drove into Wickenburg to pick up a few last-minute items from the list Greg sent.

"I think so."

Greg's laughter filled his car. "The first one is always the hardest. You don't really know what to expect until you've been there."

"You provided great info for what to pack and what to leave behind. I also watched the videos you sent a few months ago. I'm as ready as I can be."

He hoped. Tension coiled around his stomach. Nerves.

"Remember to pray. Have your family pray over you too. This is where it gets real, and we have to be mentally, emotionally, and spiritually prepared. Most folks forget the spiritual part."

That feeling in his gut tightened. He had ignored Papi's texts for the last few days. Though he made the excuse of being too busy preparing for his trip, it had been a lie. He still hadn't talked to his parents much since the big reveal. He kept burying the unease.

After he picked up the last few items from town, he drove back to the ranch. Papi's truck sat parked in front of the bunkhouse—a very unusual sight—leaving Devon no choice but to talk to his dad. He sighed before he exited his vehicle with a bag in each hand.

Papi looked up from an easy chair in the living room as Devon walked past. He stood, and Devon sensed his presence as he set his things on his bunk.

"Son."

Taking a fortifying breath, Devon turned to face Papi. Sadness etched lines in his father's face. Those blue eyes lost their twinkle. Had the past few weeks taken a toll on him, too?

"I just brewed a pot of coffee. Come sit with me for a few minutes."

Recognizing that the request was both an invitation and a command, Devon followed his father to the bunkhouse's kitchen. He fixed himself a cup of coffee with a splash of vanilla cinnamon creamer before sitting across from him.

Papi sipped his black coffee before he held Devon's gaze, much like he had when Devon had done something disappointing as a boy.

"Your mami is heartbroken that you have not come by for family supper in a month. We both thought you would make an appearance yesterday, especially since you are leaving tomorrow."

Devon raised the mug to his lips as his heart squeezed over the pain in his father's voice. Sure, Papi hadn't sired him. But he had been a true and loving father in every noble way. Devon realized now that it had been wrong for him to stay away.

Papi reached across the table and placed his hand over Devon's. Devon met his father's gaze.

"I know it was a shock to you to learn you had another set of parents."

Another set of parents. The words settled over Devon's soul. Papi said a lot with those words. He and Mami were Devon's parents. Loved him like parents ought. Raised him to love God and others. If it hadn't been for their example of showing others Jesus by trying to live like Him, Devon would not be leaving in the morning for Guatemala.

"I'm sorry," he mumbled, hiding his shame behind a gulp of coffee.

"Dev. I can only imagine how hard this has been for you. How hard it will be for your brother. But when Catalina came to me the day your mother died, and said she believed God had called us to be your parents, I knew before I prayed it was God's plan for you. And for us. He confirmed it through more prayer. Ours and our parents. Diego and Katie prayed with us, too. We knew if we were to take on the challenge, we had to treat you and Drake the same as our sons."

Papi snorted. "See? Even trying to describe the relation-ship with our oldest three sons feels weird. You are my son, Devon. Drake is my son. I love you both as much as any of the boys."

Devon's eyes burned. He had taken that love for granted while wrapped up in his own emotions.

Papi cleared his throat. "Please come to supper tonight. Mami and me want to pray over you for your trip. So do your brothers — all of them. And Padre."

Devon swallowed down the lump forming in his throat. "I'll be there."

THAT EVENING, DEVON drove over to the family ranch house. A row of familiar vehicles lined the parking area. Rennie's white Jeep. Derin's dually. Brisa's minivan. Drake's motorcycle. Mami's sedan. Papi's truck, next to Dalton's and River's. His family.

Devon eased out of his 4Runner before taking the porch stairs two at a time. He opened the door, greeted by the aroma of roasted chicken and mole. His mouth watered as his heart melted. Mami made his favorite. Roasted chicken enchiladas in her dark mole sauce. He would dream about this food while in Guatemala.

"*Mijo!*"

Mami rushed across the great room, engulfing him in a firm hug. He patted his mami's back, savoring her unconditional love for a moment. Soon, the noise of a family dinner filled the house. His brothers and their families greeted him. Papi held a chair out for him, hugging him tightly before he sat.

Then the familiar rhythm of a Vargas family meal refreshed Devon's soul. The family motto to end the blessing. Good-natured banter. Smiles and laughter.

We do not deviate from the Lord's plan. Those words rang through his mind. Papi and Mami recognized God's plan when Devon's mother died. Why hadn't he seen it before?

Lord, thank you for my family — those present and those who passed on. May we always be this close, no matter what comes. Forgive me for taking this blessing for granted. For taking them for granted. Amen.

When supper wound down, Papi gathered his brothers, Mami, and Padre in the great room while his sisters-in-law and cousins cleaned up the meal.

"Tomorrow Devon goes off to a foreign country to serve the children at a Guatemalan mission. Though none of you have left us, I would like to add a new Vargas tradition — one where we pray over those leaving."

The chatter from the kitchen silenced as the women joined the gathering.

"Devon, come here." Papi motioned him to stand between him and Mami.

"Catalina will start the prayer. I will end it. If you feel led to pray over Devon, please do so."

Then everyone bowed their heads. Devon felt the warmth of many family member's hands on his arms, shoulders, and back. Mami prayed a beautiful commission in Spanish before Padre said a few words. Then Dalton,

Dylan, Derin, and Drake all prayed for safe travels, protection, and that God would work mightily through him. By the time his sisters-in-law, cousins, and even his nephew Braden finished, tears streamed down Devon's cheeks.

Papi squeezed his shoulder, praying boldly for God's work to be completed. Then he thanked God for Devon—a son with a heart for service.

"Altogether, Vargeses."

"We do not deviate from the Lord's plan. Amen."

A holy silence fell over the room. The hairs on Devon's arms stood on end in the few seconds before his parents pulled him close for a heart-felt embrace. Each person hugged him, promising to pray for his trip.

Suddenly, two weeks apart from them seemed like forever. He swiped the dampness from his face with the back of his hands.

"*Mijo*," Mami said, pushing two containers into his hand. "Take some dessert to Raina."

Ah, his mami. Always the matchmaker.

Devon dropped a kiss on her cheek before saying his farewells. Drake promised to drive him to the airport in the morning.

Then he drove over to the women's housing. His heart thrummed in his chest as he knocked on the door. After a minute, the door creaked open.

"Devon. What brings you by?"

"I brought you some dessert. Wanna sit with me while we eat it?"

When she held the door open wider, he shook his head. "No men allowed in the women's quarters."

Her pretty green eyes rounded. She pulled the door shut behind her as she stepped onto the porch. Devon scooted a side table between two chairs. He handed her a plastic fork and one container.

"What is it?"

Devon opened it and breathed deeply. "*Tres leches* cake.

Enjoy."

Raina slid the fork into the moist cake. Devon chewed a bite of his own as he watched her reaction. Her eyelids flitted shut as a soft moan escaped her throat. Then those green eyes appeared again.

"This is so good."

"It's my favorite. Everything Mami makes tastes good. But this is the best."

"I have to agree. It *is* the best."

A blob of icing nestled against the corner of her mouth. Devon held his breath. Then he reached out and swiped his finger over it before offering the icing dot to her. Her soft lips captured his finger, cleaning away the icing and igniting the air between them.

He stood, taking the container from her hands and setting it on the table. Then he pulled her against his chest, cupping her face with his hand. He hesitated only long enough to read her consent before he moved his lips over hers with little restraint.

RAINA'S BREATH HITCHED right before Devon's lips melded with hers. Warm, inviting motion deepened, drawing her heart closer to his. The sweet taste of the tres leches cake lingered. His hand lodged in her hair before his lips moved down her neck. He rubbed a curl of her hair between his thumb and forefinger before continuing his trail of kisses.

"Mmm. It is soft."

The heady feeling of his touch and his kisses filled a hole in her heart. She redirected his mouth back to hers, returning the heated kiss move for move. A groan rumbled through his chest right before he dropped his hands to her waist and slowed the kiss to a sweet end.

Raina gazed into his green eyes, which had turned to a

dark emerald in the growing dusk. He ran a finger along her cheek before tapping it lightly on her nose.

"I'm gonna miss you, Raina Crawford."

Miss her? Oh, his trip. He was leaving in the morning. The thought knifed through her. After such a kiss, could he really leave her?

She stepped back, wrapping her arms around her middle. Kissing him like that had been a mistake. Just like everyone else she had opened her heart to, Devon would leave her behind.

"Raina. It's two weeks."

His husky voice did little to calm her fears.

"I'll be back before you know it."

Her head snapped up to meet his gaze. "That's what my parents said."

She darted toward the door of her home.

"Raina," Devon pleaded. His hand ran down her arm to the doorknob. He held it firmly shut.

"Look at me."

Raina lifted her chin. "You can't... You can't kiss me like that and then leave."

"Oh, sweetheart. I'm sorry. I didn't think."

She allowed him to turn her toward him. His comforting arms wrapped around her while one hand stroked her soft curls. She buried her face against his warm chest as her hands slipped around his middle.

"I only wanted to express how much I've come to care for you. I... My timing is bad. I'm sorry."

"Don't leave me." Her voice sounded irrationally desperate. He must think her crazy.

"Raina. I'll be back in two weeks. We can talk about us more."

With a finger under her chin, he nudged her face up. "I will think of you every day."

A sniffle shuttered inside her. She would miss him so much. Even more now that he had kissed her like that. Oh, that she could overcome her fears born out of the pain of her past. She knew he didn't intend to leave her for good. But it still tore her heart into pieces. A goodbye kiss that sent her thoughts and fears into overdrive.

"You should go."

She pressed her palm on Devon's chest, pushing him away. His fingers brushed slowly down her arm until he clasped her hands.

"I will, but not until you look at me."

Raina finally did.

"I care for you. And I'm coming back."

She nodded, swallowing down the lump constricting her throat.

"I am."

He squeezed her hands before releasing them. Then he backed away, watching her until he climbed into his vehicle.

Raina darted inside, running to her room. She flopped down on her bed as the sobs shook her body. She had done it now. Gone and fallen in love with Devon. He might be leaving her for two weeks now. But when he learned her secret, she would lose him forever. She knew it as surely as she knew her own name.

11

DEVON SIGHED AS he boarded the plane for Guatemala City behind Greg. Their team included six men and women from Arizona, besides a few more people from other states. In that moment, he still couldn't believe he was actually doing this.

The idea came a few years ago. First, during his quiet time reading his Bible and praying. Then he met Greg, an old friend from high school, for lunch. Greg had just started with the organization that specialized in teaching kids in impoverished countries about Jesus. They partnered with food, medical, and construction outreach programs. Greg had just returned from a poor town in Guatemala, more on fire for God than Devon had ever seen him.

Devon was no expert on understanding the will of God, but he knew if he kept asking, God would make his path clear. So he learned about the organization, took their program to learn how to best minister to kids from different cultures and socioeconomic situations. He practiced speaking Spanish more often, which made Mami proud. And he met with Greg once a month to pray and plan for this day.

It had finally arrived. He tossed his backpack in the overhead compartment, kicking a smaller collapsible bag under the seat in front of him as he eased into the window seat. His knees knocked against the back of the seat in front of him. Greg plopped onto the middle seat while Greg's girlfriend, Caitlyn, sat on the aisle seat.

"Hey, you want to trade with Caitlyn?" Greg asked, offering him the aisle seat.

"I'm good. First time flying."

"Really?"

Devon shrugged. "Never needed to go anywhere before."

His leg bobbed up and down as the plane backed out from the gate. When they took off, he watched out the window, glad he'd sat there for his first flight. The Phoenix metro area shrank as they gained altitude and it quickly disappeared behind them.

Lord, You've been preparing us for this trip for a long time. Let us be Your hands and feet to the community You place us in. Give us the words to speak and hearts submitted to you. Amen.

During the flight, he popped in some earbuds and watched a movie on his phone. Before he knew it, they were on the ground in a foreign country.

Excitement and apprehension flooded his senses as he stepped outside onto the curb. The city looked like any other city he had visited, with paved streets and noise everywhere. He stuck close to Greg and Caitlyn as they headed toward a taxi. They drove outside the city to a small town where they ate a hot meal before catching a bus to their final destination.

"How long is the bus ride?" he asked.

"Between two and six hours. Depends on the condition of the roads."

The air thickened, noticeably more humid than the desert climate Devon had lived in all his life. Tall palm trees, heavy brush and plant growth, and narrow dusty roads spread out before them. In the distance, he could make out a mountain. As the road wound higher, the far side of the bus hugged a steep drop-off. Devon was glad he hadn't sat on that side.

The old bus jostled and jolted over deep ruts and hard

bumps. He forced his body to loosen, knowing he'd be sore if he tried to keep himself steady. A low growl from the engine sputtered as the driver slowed the vehicle, grinding the complaining gears. A rather large split in the road caused everyone to bounce off their seats. He nearly hit his head on the ceiling.

By the time they arrived at the village, Devon could hardly wait to get off the bus. As soon as he stepped down from the vehicle, bugs pricked his skin, looking for their meal. A shiver ran down his spine as he dropped his backpack to the ground, retrieved his bug repellent lotion, and applied it liberally to his exposed skin, except for his face. Though it tempted him.

"I always knew you were sweet," Caitlyn teased as he dropped the lotion in his bag.

"Funny."

The family who ran the center took them on a tour. "We have a few mattresses in this room, but not enough for everyone."

Devon didn't mind. Greg warned him that might happen, so he had packed a thin travel mat. So far, he had been glad he packed exactly what Greg had recommended. Of course, part of Greg's job was to prepare the volunteers for the trip. They stowed their backpacks before touring the rest of the property.

Short thatched huts stood bordering the outer perimeter, nestled near the tall palm trees and jungle forest overgrowth. A wide grassy area spread out before them. Children's giggles floated in the air. They spoke in rapid fire Spanish as they swarmed the team.

"What is your name?" one little girl with a bright pink shirt asked, tugging on his cargo pant leg.

"Devon. What is yours?"

"Felipa."

Devon crouched down to her level. Speaking in Spanish, he said, "That's a pretty shirt."

Her face brightened with her gap-toothed smile. She clasped her hands behind her and twisted from side to side, skirt swaying from the movement as she angled her head down. Devon thought he might love the little girl already.

She quickly recovered from her bashfulness and introduced him to her many friends. Devon associated their names with something about them. Felipa the bold. Nery, the very young girl with her thumb stuck in her mouth. Mario the macho, with his little chest puffed out, and wary eyes. Smart kid. Rolando the funny.

The warm sun illuminated the bright colors of the children's clothing. Others joined them, giggling and chattering, accompanied by the sound of jungle insects in the background. The humid air smelled lush compared to his desert home. A cloud floated overhead, briefly casting a shadow over the lawn before moving on.

When Mario asked if he knew how to play football, he nodded, almost forgetting that football everywhere else was the same as US soccer. Thankfully, he knew that, too. The boys gathered around him and kicked a well-worn soccer ball in the middle of their group. Devon glanced at Greg to make sure he wasn't needed elsewhere. Greg joined them, allaying any of Devon's concerns.

"It's about building relationships on their level. Time means very little here. The more you go with the flow, the more you'll connect with them."

Devon grinned when Rolando kicked the ball his way. Devon dribbled it briefly before sending it sailing toward another boy. The shy kid's face lit up as he ran with the ball until another boy stole it away. The shy kid's giggles filled Devon's heart with joy. Even though he had just arrived, he was glad he came.

An hour later, with a passel of merry children circled around him, Devon helped serve food to them. Then Greg asked him if he would share one of the Bible stories they had prepared. For some reason, the story about Zacchaeus came to mind. The moment he began speaking, all the children quieted and stared at him with rapt attention. He realized that the simple act of telling them a story in their own language was a privilege. He shot a quick prayer for the right words as he spoke.

"Once upon a time, there was a man named Zacchaeus. He worked as a tax collector — meaning he took money from people to give to a rich man who ruled the land."

"One day, Jesus came to his town. The crowds gathered around him and Zacchaeus could not see Jesus. He was a short man."

Devon motioned his hand to emphasize his point. An unbidden thought of a short, curly haired woman flashed in his mind. He pushed the thoughts of her away as he continued.

"Zacchaeus wanted to see Jesus, so what do you think he did?"

"Oh, I know!"

Devon nodded to the little boy.

"He climbed a mountain!"

"No."

Nery raised her hand. "He climbed on top of his house?"

"No. He climbed up a tree so he could see him." Devon acted it out, finishing with a hand resting above his eyes, leaning forward as if searching across a great distance.

Round eyes flashed with understanding.

"When Jesus passed by the tree, he looked up and told Zacchaeus to come down and that he wanted to have dinner with him."

"How did he know Zacchaeus was there?" Rolando asked.

"Because Jesus is God's son. He knows everything."

"More than abuela?" Mario asked.

Devon laughed. "Yes, more than your abuela."

"What did he do?" Felipa asked.

"Well, he climbed down the tree and hosted dinner. But

some people in town didn't like that Jesus went to Zacchaeus's home, because of his job."

Nery pouted. "That's sad."

"But Jesus told them he came to seek and save the lost."

Greg took over, explaining a little more about Jesus to the kids. Then they sang a song together. When it finished, Felipa the bold shouted out a question.

"Devon? Does Jesus love tall people too?"

He crouched in front of her. "Yes, Felipa. He loves all people. Short and tall and everything in between."

"Good. My uncle is tall. And so are you."

Devon laughed. "Don't worry," he said as he gave her a side hug. "Jesus and I are old friends."

"He takes care of me."

"Who?"

"My uncle. My mami and papi died."

The words from the brave child caused Devon's eyes to sting. "My mami and papi died too. My aunt and uncle raised me."

The lump in his throat choked out any further words he wanted to say. Felipa wrapped her arms around his neck and squeezed tight.

"Jesus loves you, too," she said before she released him.

Caitlyn took the stage, strumming her guitar. She led the children in *Jesus Loves Me*. Devon coughed and snuck out of the center, swallowing back the emotion.

Yes, Jesus loved him. And Mami and Papi's love and care were proof of it.

He snorted. It was only the first day and already, his heart felt stripped down to the core. He could only imagine what the coming days would hold.

A WEEK AFTER Devon left for the mission trip, Raina

woke with a heavy sense of trepidation. She couldn't shake it, so she prayed for him as often as he came to mind.

By midafternoon, her concentration waned. She stared at the computer on her desk, not really seeing what was before her.

"Hey." Renata's voice drew her attention. "Settling in okay?"

Raina nodded. "Yeah. I'm so glad Devon trained me. I feel more confident about everything."

"Have you heard from him?"

"No. You?"

Renata shook her head. "I'll ask Aunt Catalina later."

"I was thinking I'd like to set up an area for the older kids to work on a puzzle together," Raina said. "But I want to divide the space differently so the littles won't be able to wander around so much. I'd hate for them to find a puzzle piece and put it in their mouths."

"I'll ask some cowboys to help. When do you want them?"

"Tomorrow morning?"

"Sounds good. Anything else like that, we'll want to finish in the next two weeks. The season starts in three."

"That's the only major change. Everything else, me and the care workers can handle."

"Excellent. I'll let you know what Aunt Catalina says."

Raina's cheeks heated. She wanted to know how Devon fared. Yet, did she have any right to ask? He kissed her once. It's not like they were a couple or anything.

Oh, what a kiss it had been. One that kept her awake at night, reliving it. Along with his promise to talk about "us" when he returned.

The next morning, her mind kept going to Devon. Was his trip everything he had hoped? Were the kids learning about Jesus? Was he having fun?

She tried to force thoughts of Devon from her mind as she sat down at her computer. All the employees' kids were at a horse clinic or stayed home, so she had time to plan and rearrange things. About a half hour later, someone knocked on the doorframe of her office.

"Morning, Raina."

She stared at the cowboy, trying to place his name. He was several inches shorter than Devon. His shiny buckle caught her attention. PBR. Oh, that's right, he had been a pro bull rider.

"Adan, right?"

"Yes, ma'am. This is Ross. Rennie said you have a construction project that needs attention."

Raina laughed. "Yeah, sorta."

She motioned him out to the main room. "I'd like to offer some different activities for the more introverted older kids. Things like a one-thousand piece puzzle. I'm worried about the littles wandering around, picking up pieces..."

"I can see your dilemma."

"I'd like a short wall, one we can easily see over, that will define the space for one to three-year-olds. I'd like some sort of latching short door, but nothing that will pinch fingers."

"I could put one of those sliding latches on the outside. Easy for adults to reach, but out of reach for toddlers."

"That's brilliant."

They continued to plan the space with Raina asserting that she wanted the wall to be short so they'd have an easy line of sight. Adan suggested adding plexiglass above the wall for another two feet to keep them from climbing over it. Ross took measurements and jotted them down on paper. Then the two of them headed out for supplies.

When they returned, they set up shop outside, under an awning but close to the children's center. Adan assured her they could complete construction that day and come back to paint and move furniture the next day.

An idea came to mind. She would paint some bright animals on the wall in the toddler area. Maybe butterflies and bugs. She grabbed her notebook and sketched a few simple outlines, including a cat, dog, and bird to go with the butterflies. While the men worked, she found Renata in the resort office to tell her the plan.

"Oh! I'd love to go shopping with you. It's so dead around here. Let's you and me go together?"

Raina smiled, thrilled that her roommate and boss actually wanted to hang out with her. It shouldn't surprise her, though. Over the past few weeks at the ranch, the two often chatted in the evening, getting to know each other better.

Renata glanced at her watch. "We can stop at *The Lariat* for lunch before shopping. My treat."

Since Renata offered to drive, Raina hopped into her Jeep Wrangler. She barely buckled her seatbelt by the time Renata backed out of the spot. The scent of an apple cinnamon air freshener helped Raina feel more comfortable.

"Aunt Catalina said she's received a few texts from Devon. He sent a picture of this sweet gap-toothed little girl that adopted him. Her name is Felipa."

"Such a pretty name."

"My aunt said he keeps asking about you."

Raina's stomach tightened, and her shoulders sagged. "Probably worried that I might burn the place down."

Renata frowned. "Not at all. He is extremely pleased with the work you're doing. He even expressed that it's a beneficial thing for him to move on. You can do a far superior job compared to him."

Raina straightened in her seat. "Really?"

"Yes. Besides, I'm pretty sure he asks about you because he misses you."

Renata parked the Jeep on a quaint street before cutting the engine. Heat warmed Raina's face as she stepped onto the curb.

"You miss him, too, don't you?"

Raina figured there was no point denying it. "Yeah. He's been on my mind since he left. Since the..."

Renata turned toward her. "The?"

Raina reached for the black metal handle on the glass door and yanked it open. When she stepped inside the café, she stopped. Chalkboard paint covered the wall across from the entrance with neatly written menu items. Almost too neat. Raina wondered if they used some sort of stencils. It gave her an idea to paint a chalkboard wall in the children's center for the kindergarten to second graders. How fun would that be?

The café reminded her of a French bistro with touches of western flair. The knotty pine wood bar gleamed under the tear-drop shaped hanging lights. Pops of yellow and red brightened the space. Booths lined one side of the restaurant, while tables with black wrought-iron chairs filled the rest of it. Classic western music played softly in the background. The aroma of fresh food and coffee made Raina's stomach grumble.

Everything about the place welcomed her. Stunning photos of western men, women, couples, and kids lined several walls. One picture with a sense of familiarity drew her attention. The cowboy wore a dark brown hat similar to Devon's. He was tall, and something about his prominent chin reminded her of Devon.

"I see you spotted his picture," Renata said, leading her over to it. "It's from a few years ago. Cara had been out at the ranch shooting scenery and stopped by the resort office to ask if we needed any art refreshed. She's Greta's, the café owner's niece. When we drove over to the stable, we spotted Devon. He stood outside with his arms propped on a corral fence, one foot on the bottom rung, watching the horses. It's quintessential Devon. Deep in thought. Mind always working."

Raina studied the photo, while Renata stepped away to talk to Greta. Though the shadow from his hat obscured part of his face, she could see what Renata said. His mind had been churning. She wondered if it ever rested. If he ever rested.

An urgent sense to pray for him pressed on her heart. *Lord, please be with Devon. Keep him safe. Bring him home whole and healthy.* Odd. Unsure why those particular words came forth, she finished the prayer.

Her gaze dropped to the price of the photo. While not cheap, she could afford to splurge on it. Would it be dumb to have a picture of him hanging in her room? What if nothing came out of their time together? What if he wanted nothing to do with her after he returned?

Raina sighed and joined Renata at a table, resolving to think about it more before purchasing the picture.

"What about you?" Raina asked Renata while they waited for their sandwiches. "Any special someone?"

Renata's smile faded. "No. The resort keeps me busy. And I don't date cowboys."

"Cowboys that work for your family or all cowboys?"

"All."

"Sounds like there's a story there."

Renata's shoulders lifted and fell with her heavy intake of air. "Yeah. We'll save it for some other time."

Then her eyes flashed with mirth. "You know who would love to take part in our mural project?"

Raina shook her head.

"Devon. I'm sure he'll be sad to miss it, but I say we go big to make him jealous."

Raina laughed at Renata's silliness. She enjoyed making friends.

THE NEXT DAY, Adan and Ross repainted the entire room, not just the new short walls. The following day, Solana joined Renata and Raina for the mural project. Raina sketched the outline of the critters in the toddler's cove while

Adan and Taylor painted the chalkboard wall. Raina noticed how often Solana's gaze followed the pair.

"Lanni!" Renata exclaimed. "You're dripping."

"Oh!" Solana grabbed a rag to wipe up the dribble of yellow paint that ran down from the cat. "I'm so sorry."

"Not to worry," Raina said. "We'll touch up with the wall color. Or I'll add some whimsical lines to cover it up."

"What is with you today, anyway?" Renata asked her sister.

Solana's cheeks flamed. "Nothing."

"You like Adan." Raina wished she would have thought about it before blurting out her observation.

"Do you?" Renata asked.

Solana's gaze dropped to the cat. She sponged on some rust to create the illusion of fur. "Maybe."

After she expelled a loud breath, she moved on to the next animal.

"I mean, look at him. Taylor is young enough to be his daughter."

"And?" Renata nudged. "It's not like he's seeing anyone."

"He's not?" Solana's face transformed into a mix of joy and hope.

Raina ducked her chin behind her shoulder, so Solana wouldn't see her smile.

"How old is he?" Raina quickly added, "Asking for a friend."

Renata's loud guffaw drew Adan's attention, causing Solana to look away while her cheeks flushed bright red. When Renata's laughter subsided, she finally answered.

"Adan is thirty-three now, I think. A solid decade older than you, Lanni."

Solana huffed before she turned her attention to painting brown spots on the dog. "It's not like he would ever notice me, anyway."

Raina looked at Renata, who widened her eyes and tilted her head. Then Raina mouthed, *what's that about?* Renata shrugged. Seemed like her other roommate had a giant crush on one former pro bull rider. Interesting.

A few hours later, Raina stood admiring the new space. She'd even stenciled the letters to spell out "Toddler's Cove" between the whimsical critters she created.

"It looks amazing," Renata said before snapping several pictures with her phone. Then she texted someone. "I told Aunt Catalina to stop by. She'll love it."

"Thanks."

Raina studied their work. Wide-eyed, smiling animals created a welcoming scene. The bright colors popped against the neutral background. When she started her center for orphans, she would do the same thing. Create a happy, inviting home—one that would heal the hurts of the children. Gratitude for the opportunity to use her talents for others filled her heart.

Then Raina took a few pictures of her own. She wished Devon had been there. She would have enjoyed sharing the moment with him.

12

DEVON WOKE ABRUPTLY, interrupted by a piercing ache in his side. The sharp and relentless sensation caused his stomach to churn, unleashing an overwhelming surge of nausea. Waves of discomfort washed over him, leaving him trembling uncontrollably and drenched in perspiration. In a feeble attempt to find relief, he instinctively curled up into a tight ball, his moans escaping from deep within his suffering body.

"Devon?" Greg stood over him with water and a chewable antacid. "Take this."

His eyes fluttered shut as he shook his head. Big mistake. The dizziness caused his stomach to lurch. Bile rose in this throat as he shot to his feet. He slammed his palm against the wall for balance, the rough texture scraping against his skin as he made his way outside. Once the cool, humid air hit his face, he spewed the contents of his stomach over the railing. He heaved again. Then he went limp, half hugging the wooden railing of the porch. It took too much effort to stand up. Or move.

"Please try to take this. I promise it will help."

Devon sipped the offered warm water, swishing it in his mouth before spitting it out. He placed the chalky tablet on his tongue and chewed it slowly. After he washed it down with water, he slumped to the hard floor. Sitting partly upright took too much strength, so he flopped onto his side.

"Is anyone else sick?" Greg asked.

"No," Caitlyn answered. "I think it's just Devon. Poor thing."

"Help me get him to the medical building."

Devon barely registered his friend's hands, hauling him to his feet. Both Caitlyn and Greg looped an arm around Devon's waist. He stumbled forward awkwardly, only partially aware of his surroundings. It seemed like they walked three miles before they let him lay down again. He closed his eyes as shivers shook his body.

Everything hurt. His joints. His head. His stomach. It felt like someone impaled him with a sword.

"This isn't dehydration. Maybe a parasite," an unfamiliar female voice said.

"But?"

"Does he still have his appendix?" The doctor's voice faded. "Could be appendicitis."

"Are you serious?" Caitlyn's shrill voice broke through Devon's fog.

Great. Just great. The last thing he needed was to have surgery in the middle of a jungle village. While on a mission trip. How long would it take to heal from it? Would he get an infection? And seriously, why did God bring him all the way here for his appendix to act up? He was doing a good thing, ministering to the kids.

"Have you given him anything?"

"Just an antacid," Greg said.

Pain radiated through his side. When it eased, he told the doctor it hadn't helped.

"Devon, please roll onto your back. Let me examine you."

Sweat dripped into his eyes as he shifted. Everything took too much effort. As another stabbing pain sliced through his right side, he clenched his jaw.

The doctor listened to his heart and his breathing. Then she pressed on different parts of his abdomen. When she touched his right side below his rib cage, almost to his hip, he let out a yelp.

"We need to get him back to Guatemala City ASAP. He needs some imaging to confirm my diagnosis, but I'm fairly certain he has appendicitis."

Devon rolled onto his side and curled into a ball against the severe pain as Greg stepped from the room. He wasn't sure how long his friend had been gone. When he returned, he said he had a Jeep waiting. Then he and another man from their group helped him into the back.

"Hang in there, buddy."

Greg slid into the passenger seat as the owner of the Jeep shifted into gear. The motion of the vehicle made Devon woozy. He thought he might be dying it hurt so much.

A few times on the drive to the city, they stopped so Devon could vomit. During the last time he threw up, Greg climbed into the back seat, plying Devon with water. In any other situation, it would be awkward to rest his head in his friend's lap.

When they finally entered the hospital, the sterile smell of disinfectant filled the air. The sight of bustling nurses and doctors rushing by added a sense of urgency. The sounds of beeping machines and muffled conversations created a cacophony in the background. Devon felt a mix of relief and anxiety, grateful for Greg's unwavering presence. Thankfully, Greg had brought his things, including his cell phone. He needed to let Mami and Papi know about the situation.

The pain muddled his brain, causing Devon to float between oblivion and awareness. Surely they would give him something for the pain soon. His body felt like it was on fire, burning from one annoying organ. Nausea doubled him over before someone thrust a bedpan under his mouth. When he started to collapse, someone lifted him onto a bed. At last, a nurse began hooking him up to monitoring devices while several men talked nearby.

"Surgery..."

"Can we transport him home?" The anxiety in Greg's voice echoed in the confined space.

"I'd advise against it."

"Dev?" Greg's face appeared over him. "The doctor says they need to remove your appendix. Will you consent to surgery?"

Devon nodded. He'd consent to anything that would stop the intense pain.

"Sir, we need verbal agreement."

"Yes." He forced the word through his pursed lips.

Silence for a moment. Then chilly hands pawed at him. A jab in his arm followed by liquid flowing into his veins. Sleepiness beckoned him before Devon called out for Greg.

"Mami. Papi."

"Already called them. They are on their way."

Devon's eyes burned. Before he slipped from consciousness, he thanked God for his wonderful parents. They were coming. Everything would be alright.

Raina had left the door open from her office to the resort reception area to air out the room. The fresh paint odor still hung in the air the day after they completed the renovation.

"I have to go to him, Rennie." Catalina's voice sounded full of fear. "He's having surgery."

"Oh, my! In Guatemala?" Renata asked.

Raina stood in the doorway as soon as she realized they were talking about Devon. Catalina's grim expression worried her. Renata motioned her to join them.

"What happened?" she asked.

"Appendix," Renata answered.

"Is it safe for him to have surgery there?"

"Ay. They transported him to Guatemala City. To a reputable hospital."

"We should pray for him," Raina suggested.

Renata, Solana, Catalina, and Raina gathered in a circle. They prayed for the surgeons and Devon. Then they prayed for safe travels for Tres and Catalina, and for a quick recovery.

The sound of a man clearing his throat came from the doorway. "Are you ready, Cat?"

Tres Vargas stood in the doorway, face pale and with deep creases in his forehead. Raina offered a silent prayer for him, too.

"Dalton's waiting to take us to the airport."

"Si. Please keep praying for him," Catalina said over her shoulder before she left.

"Appendecitis. How random?" Solana muttered.

Raina nodded numbly. This couldn't be happening. Just as she opened her heart to the possibility of loving someone, he might die. A sob escaped her throat unbidden.

Renata and Solana wrapped her in a group hug, praying for her.

"Trust God, Raina. Devon will come home safely. I know it."

"Yeah," Solana added. "We must have faith."

Raina wiped the tears from her eyes. "Can you let Josh and Amber know I'm going to take a long lunch in town?"

"Will do," Renata said.

Raina retrieved her purse from her office before sliding behind the wheel of her beat up old car. Then she headed into Wickenburg to *The Lariat*.

Once inside, she asked for a table where she could look at the picture of Devon. *Oh, Lord! Please keep him safe. I'm not ready to say goodbye to anyone else. I know I shouldn't care so much for him so soon, but I do. Please heal his body. Bring him home to Vargas Ranch.*

When Greta brought her salad, she placed a hand on Raina's shoulder.

"Are you alright, Raina?"

She shook her head. Despite the lunchtime crowd, Greta pulled out the seat across from her and listened.

"I think I'm falling for Devon Vargas and he's stuck in a hospital in Guatemala."

Greta reached across the table and squeezed her hand. "Perhaps you should start at the beginning."

By the time she finished telling Greta all about it, the place had cleared out. It was then Raina realized Greta had two other servers working. She felt a little relieved knowing she hadn't hurt the kind, older woman's business.

"Thanks for listening."

"Anytime, dear."

"Greta, I'd like to buy that picture, if it's okay."

"Of course. Let me ring it up for you."

Raina dug her debit card from her purse and handed it to the motherly woman. Then Greta cleaned the glass and frame before taking it down from the wall. She brought back both the picture and Raina's card.

"I'll be praying for Devon. And for you."

"Thanks!"

Later that evening, Renata helped her hang the picture in her room on the wall across from her bed. Raina felt a little embarrassed, but Renata assured her it made sense she had purchased it.

Before she turned out the lights for the night, she stared at the picture of her smart cowboy, praying for his body. Then she flipped off the light and burrowed under the covers, hoping sleep would come soon.

13

DEVON TRIED TO move his arms, but they each felt as if they weighed one thousand pounds. He blinked his eyes open a few times, adjusting to the bright, unfamiliar room. A steady beeping came from nearby. He couldn't place the familiar sound. Soft fingers brushed a lock of his hair from his forehead.

"Ma..." Mami.

His dry mouth felt full of cotton.

"*Mijo*, don't try to talk. The nurse will get you some water soon."

The loud ripping of velcro echoed in the room before someone lifted his arm and gently let it settle on the bed again. He glanced over and saw a nurse rolling up the cord of the blood pressure cuff. She checked the other equipment before quietly exiting the room.

Mami pressed the button on his bed, causing it to angle him partially upright.

Then it hit Devon. He was still in Guatemala. How was Mami there?

"Here, *mijo*, sip this."

Mami held a straw to his parched lips. He swallowed a small sip, the warm water noticeably sluicing down his esophagus to his stomach. No doubt about it, he felt weird. When she suggested another sip, he shook his head.

"What. Happened?"

Mami's eyes reddened. "We almost lost you."

Devon swallowed away the lump in his throat as he waited for her to continue.

"Your appendix almost ruptured. God brought you to the hospital just in time…" Mami tried to stifle a snob-snort. She squared her shoulders and sucked in a loud breath. "They removed your appendix. You'll recover soon. That is all that matters now."

"How. You. Here?"

"Greg called us and we hopped on the first flight here."

"We?"

"Papi's here. Out talking to the doctor to see when we can fly you home."

The thought of sitting upright in an airplane made him want to throw up. Not that he felt any pain in that moment. Just extremely uncomfortable. The flying process — security lines, luggage, sitting for hours — that sounded like a horrible idea.

"He's also trying to see if we can charter a private flight home."

"Expensive." He protested.

"Oh, *mijo*." Mami squeezed his hand. "No cost is too great to bring you home."

Devon's eyes watered, spilling onto his cheeks. Must be the pain meds making him overly sensitive. Mami leaned over with a tissue, drying his wet face. Then she pressed her lips to his forehead for several seconds.

"Try to rest more."

Devon closed his eyes and let sleep claim him again.

THROUGHOUT THE DAY, Devon wavered between sleep and consciousness. Papi helped him get out of bed and walk down the hall, per the nurse's orders, each time he woke. At first, every movement seemed to take an enormous amount of effort. By the second afternoon, it grew easier.

After one walk, while Mami left to get supper in the cafeteria, Devon finally braved a question to his papi.

"Tell me about them. Devon and Anita."

Papi eased onto the guest chair before wiping a hand over his face.

"All three of us boys were close growing up. I was the responsible one, much like Dalton."

"I figured."

"Devon was a bit of a daredevil. Kinda like Drake acts like he wants to be. Diego was socially popular, the typical youngest. We were each two years apart."

Papi looked out the window, his voice sounding far away.

"Padre taught us to rely on family. Even when one of us wanted to stretch his independent wings, we were brothers. A bond not easily broken or ignored. We worked the cattle together. Mended fences—literal and proverbial—together. When someone came after us for any reason, we remained Vargas strong. People knew we would give the shirt off our backs to help a neighbor. They also knew if they had a beef with one of us, they would face off against all of us."

Papi's gaze connected with his.

"It's the same lesson I tried to instill in the five of you."

Devon nodded. "You did, Papi."

"Good. Just because blood made you cousins doesn't mean that life didn't make the five of you brothers. Stay strong together."

"Yes, sir."

The door creaked open and Papi shot to his feet to grab the food containers from Mami. Devon's mouth watered over the aroma of mashed potatoes and brown gravy. Wasn't sure he cared for much else. After his parents prayed over him and the food, they settled onto the two chairs in the room.

"Rennie said Raina has asked about you four times today."

A smile quirked the side of his mouth as he swallowed a tiny spoonful of food.

"Maybe I'll call her after supper."

Mami flashed him a knowing grin. Truth was, as his fog lifted, he thought about Raina several times. And their parting kiss.

He frowned.

"Something wrong, son?"

Devon quickly softened his features. "Just thinking."

When he didn't elaborate, his parents spoke softly to each other. Sounded like they made plans to fly him home.

His thoughts returned to Raina. He didn't understand how she filled so much space in his mind and heart so quickly. Even now, he couldn't picture a future without her in it. Seemed foolish on the surface.

Yet, he almost died. Died before finding a wife or having children. He and Drake were the last of their branch of the family. It was up to him to see that line continue. And suddenly, Devon no longer wanted to delay that part of his life. What difference did a career make if he didn't share his life with family — one of his own?

A plan began to form in his mind. There had been enough of a connection with Raina that if he nurtured it, it could grow into more. The chemistry was there. The spiritual like-mindedness. The friendship. All of it could mature into something lasting.

He needed to see her face. Talk to her.

"Mami, have you seen my phone?"

She stood, tossing her empty container in the trash. Then she bent over and unplugged it from the wall before handing it to him.

"Would you mind giving me some privacy?" he asked as he scrolled to Raina's contact info.

Mami's eyes widened. Papi chuckled as he stood and

tossed his food container. "Come on, Cat. Let's go grab a coffee."

Then he led her from the room, closing the door behind him.

Devon pressed the video call button before realizing he might not look so great. He hadn't seen himself in a mirror. He probably looked a fright. Hopefully Raina wouldn't mind.

When her face appeared on the screen, Devon's heart filled to overflowing. Her beautiful green eyes softened as a smile stretched across her face. His pulse quickened as he studied her for a minute. Yeah, he needed this. Just seeing her on the screen made him want to heal faster so he could get back home to her.

RAINA JUMPED UP from the couch and ducked into her bedroom when she saw the caller id. Devon.

Her heart raced as she scurried onto her bed, propping the pillows behind her. Then she answered his request for a video call. She bit her lower lip as she studied his pale face. Dark circles under his green eyes. A thick beard covered his cheeks, chin, and upper lip, giving him a bit of the mountain-man look. Nice.

"Hey."

The sound of his voice wrapped around her heart, sending it soaring. Whatever worry she felt a moment ago vanished in light of his warm, almost intimate one-word greeting.

"Hey."

Neither spoke for several seconds, so she started the conversation.

"I like the beard."

His deep laughter lifted her mood higher.

"I'm glad. I was thinking about keeping it."

She shrugged. "It's your face."

"I care about what you think. Wouldn't want it to scratch you. You know, if I were to kiss you again."

The memory of their only kiss sent butterflies dancing through her middle.

"Devon Vargas, are you flirting with me?"

His bright white teeth flashed in a heart-flipping grin, sending those butterfly wings fluttering wildly. She might just be falling for him.

"Depends. Do you like it?"

Raina rolled her eyes.

"You do."

She sighed and shifted the conversation to his health. "How are you?"

"Better, now that I can see your beautiful face."

"I'll bet you say that to all the girls." Her cheeks warmed. Was she flirting with him now?

"What other girls?"

Raina blew out a loud breath. The seriousness of his tone said far more than his words. She sensed something had changed in him. Maybe between them, too.

"So… How did you go from teaching kids about Jesus to landing in the hospital?"

Devon expelled a loud burst of air. "Seems my appendix decided to act up. Guess Greg got me to the hospital in Guatemala City just in time."

"I'm glad."

He snorted. "Me too. Anyway, they removed it. Got a cool scar about yea big on my abdomen."

Raina's face heated as he held up his thumb and forefinger about three inches apart.

"The doctor said they would normally take it out laparoscopically, but my case was an emergency. So he apologized for the long incision. Can you imagine? Like I care about a scar. The man saved my life."

Raina's eyes burned. She hadn't realized how close she had come to losing him.

"Hey, sweetheart, don't cry. I'm fine. Gonna fully recover."

That was the second time he called her sweetheart. She swiped at the tear rolling down her cheek and sat up a little straighter.

"Good."

"Tell me about your day."

"I think we're ready for the season. Of course, it's my first, so I'm not really sure what to expect."

"Mami said you made a few big changes already. Redesigned the room. Added some beautiful murals. You never told me you were an artist."

Her face heated again. Maybe it bothered him she had changed so much already. "I hope you don't mind—"

"Raina, stop trying to apologize for doing your job. Rennie and Mami are thrilled with what you've done. I trust you completely."

She captured her lip between her teeth.

Devon angled his head down. "Raina. Whatever is going on in that big, beautiful brain of yours, you need to let it go. You are the Children's Director at Vargas Guest Ranch & Resort. A title that comes with full autonomy to run the place as you see fit. From everything my family has told me, you are as amazing as I already figured out."

"You really think I'm amazing?"

"More than amazing."

"Oh."

"And I can't wait to see what you've done with the place in person. Mami said the pictures don't do it justice."

"When are you coming home?" And would he stay? Or did he still plan to move off the ranch and leave her behind? All questions she didn't have a right to ask.

"Another day or two. Once they release me from the hospital, I think Papi wants to fly me home the next day.

Mami said something about a private charter." He shook his head. "I told them not to spend so much money."

Raina swallowed away a bite of envy. What would it be like to have someone go to such extreme lengths for her? She would never know.

"Anyway, I don't think they are listening to me on this one."

When Devon yawned, Raina suggested they end the call. He placed a kiss on two of his fingers, then moved them to the camera, as if passing the kiss to her. The tender gesture melted her heart even more.

"Night, Raina."

"Night, Dev."

She caught him quirking a grin before the screen flashed black.

Ugh. She had fallen for Devon. That call solidified it. And if she wasn't mistaken, he had fallen for her.

Tell him.

The voice in her subconscious sent prickles down her spine. She needed to tell him the truth. Let him know she couldn't have children before either of them grew closer. Because if she knew anything about Devon, it was that he would want kids—kids she could never give him.

Raina's gaze traveled to the artistic photograph on the wall, studying her mysterious cowboy. Tears blurred her vision.

"Oh, Devon. Please don't hate me."

Her heart couldn't bear it.

Maybe... Maybe he would be okay with adoption.

Or maybe she could wait a little longer. If he never pursued a relationship with her, then there was no point in saying anything. She could keep her secret to herself.

Didn't he have plans to get a job teaching in the big city? Plans to leave the ranch?

Yeah, she could wait and see. No need to open that can of worms now.

14

DEVON GROANED AS he settled onto the plush leather airplane seat, still in shock over the gracious billionaire's generous use of his private jet. Guess the guy knew his sister-in-law Madison, Derin's wife. When he heard about Devon's surgery and that he'd been on a mission trip, he offered to pay for the whole thing. It could even land on the airstrip just outside of Wickenburg. No long drive from Phoenix Sky Harbor Airport.

"*Mijo*, are you in pain?" Mami asked as she dug in her purse for his medicine.

"I'm fine, Mami."

She raised one eyebrow, pursing her lips tightly. He could feel her eyes burning through him as he rested his head against the seatback. Climbing the stairs to board the plane left him more winded than it should have.

"*Mijo*—"

"Cat. Leave him alone. He'll be fine."

Devon heard Mami huff in response to his father's warning. The leather chair complained as she shifted her position.

Exhaustion tugged at him, so he missed the takeoff. They'd been in the air for a few hours by the time he opened his eyes.

"Devon, it's Raina." Papi handed him his phone.

He opened his eyes and smiled at his girlfriend. Or at

least he hoped to convince her the label fit once he arrived home.

"Hey."

"Hey."

"Are you on a plane?"

Devon nodded.

"And they let you take a call?"

He chuckled before explaining the story.

"How does Madison know a billionaire?"

"Guess she met him when she played tennis."

"Wait. She played pro tennis?"

Devon laughed. "Yeah. I'm surprised you didn't know."

"When do you land?"

He shrugged and looked up at Mami, who he knew had been listening intently to the entire conversation.

"Dos de la tarde."

"Huh?" Raina asked.

"Two p.m."

"Oh!" She waved to someone off camera. "Two o'clock. That's sooner than we thought."

Devon heard Rennie's groan in the distance. Ugh. They were up to something. He wasn't sure he had the energy for anything fussy.

"How are you feeling?"

"Tired."

"Okay. I'll let you go. See you soon."

Then she kissed her fingertips and moved them close to the camera. He smiled as he punched the end call button. He loved that the gesture had become theirs. It was the first time she had done it.

After sliding his phone into his pocket, he closed his eyes, grinning. Images of what could be scrolled in his mind. Raina bouncing a curly haired toddler on her hip. Her bustling around a modern kitchen with the best finishes his money could buy. A dog slurping gulps of water from a nearby bowl. Sunset on a patio looking over the western mountain range. His 4Runner full of kids as he drove his family to his favorite lookout — the one he had taken Raina to after their ill-fated steak dinner.

He could hardly wait to hold her in his arms again.

Maybe he would talk to Dylan about the process of building a house on the land Mami and Papi gifted him. He supposed he would need an architect and a general contractor. Dylan could put him in touch with the ones he used.

Perhaps he was getting ahead of himself. Would it be better to see if Raina felt the same first?

Ugh. His mind kept turning over the possibilities of his future. What job to take. Where to live. He needed to stop thinking about it.

"Mami."

"Si?"

"Can you tell me about Anita?"

A frown flared across her brow for a second before she expelled a loud breath.

"Si, *mijo*. Your mamacita loved you boys. She had been excited about her pregnancy with Drake. She named him as soon as she learned his gender."

Papi interjected, "She teased Cat about trying to catch up with us."

"Ay. She missed your padre fiercely. Then word came he had been killed."

Devon's eyes burned.

"It hit her hard. Spent days in bed. Eventually moved you and her into our house so we could help."

Devon cleared his throat. Not wanting to dwell on the end of her life, he asked, "How did they meet?"

Mami smiled. "Oh, *mijo*, they were so in love. Anita's family moved to Arizona during her freshman year of high school. They came for the western way of life. They lived near Scottsdale on a large horse property."

"Had an arena and the works," Papi added. "Pro reining champions trained at their facility."

"As did Anita. Though she trained for barrel racing."

"Was good at it too."

Mami rested a hand on Papi's arm. "That's how Devon met her. He had been training for team roping with his buddy. He was two years, Tres?"

"Yeah, two years ahead of Anita. A junior."

"Si. He arrived at the arena early one day and watched her barrel race. When she finished, he offered to care for her horse."

Papi laughed. "She let him, not telling him her family owned the place, and she had stable hands for that."

"Ay. And he talked to her while he groomed her horse. Then he just kept talking."

"His partner came looking for him. Missed their scheduled training time and everything."

"They started dating after that."

Devon smiled as they told the story, his birth parents becoming more real. His papi had been a team roper. His mami a barrel racer.

"Did they ever go pro?"

"No," Papi said. "They married the summer before nine-eleven. He had been set to go on the pro rodeo circuit."

When Papi's voice caught, Mami continued. "After the towers came down, he enlisted that day. Shipped out quickly."

"You were already born, I think," Papi said. "They kinda got some things out of order. You came along before the wedding."

Devon's face heated. He hoped he wasn't that much like his papi. He wanted to honor God in his relationship with Raina.

"They spent most of their marriage apart, except for the week he had leave—when Drake was conceived," Papi said.

Devon's breath hitched. "A tragic love story."

"Oh, *mijo*. They both loved you so much. And would have loved Drake had they gotten the chance to know him."

"Thank you." Devon sniffed. "For everything. For raising us. Loving us. Teaching us about God. Treating us like your own."

Mami unbuckled from her seat and crossed to him. Then she wrapped her arms around him.

"You are a son of my heart, *mijo*. I love you."

"Love you, too."

Mami dropped a kiss on his forehead before taking her seat again.

"Now, get some rest. We still have another hour before we land."

"Si, Mami."

Devon closed his eyes and drifted in and out of sleep until he noticed a change in the plane. The flight attendant came through and told them they began their descent for the landing. He wiped the grime from his eyes and sat up straighter, feeling somewhat rested.

Once on the ground, he stood and stretched, stopping short at the tenderness in his side. Better not have pulled his stitches. Papi exited first, with Devon following behind a stair or two. As he neared the bottom, Papi waited to help, if needed. Then he held Devon's elbow as he led him to Derin's truck.

"Bro!" Derin greeted him, pulling him close for a tight embrace. Devon groaned as his side ached, and Derin loosened his hold. "Thought we were gonna lose you."

He noticed Derin's throat work for a second before he helped him into the back seat. Mami sat in the other back seat, helping him with the seatbelt. Thankfully, she suggested he sit on the passenger side so the seatbelt didn't rest on his surgery site. That was just like Mami, always thinking of the little things.

Within twenty minutes, they arrived home. Derin pulled to a stop by the dining hall. Odd.

"Hang tight, little brother, and I'll help you."

"Why are we stopping here?"

Derin grinned. "I'm hungry."

Yeah, right. Something was up.

When Derin held the dining hall door open for him, tears bit the back of his eyes.

"Welcome home, Devon!" His family shouted at once.

His eyes scanned the crowd. Padre sat in a chair at the long table. Dalton stood behind him, next to River. Dylan stepped away from Braden and a very pregnant Brisa. She had to be due any day now. Before Devon finished cataloging the crowd, Dylan engulfed him in a hug.

"Good to s-s-see you."

"You too."

Drake shifted from foot to foot, impatiently waiting his turn. "You scared us."

Devon heard the quaver in his voice before Dalton hugged him.

As Dalton said something along the same lines, Devon's gaze landed on Raina. He brushed past his brother and strode directly toward her. Then he held out his hands. She did the same, so he clasped them in his for a heartbeat. Then he tugged, guiding her head to his chest, relishing the feel of her soft hair in his hand. When she wrapped her arms around his waist, he hummed.

"I don't want to hurt you." Her muffled words warmed his heart.

He bent down as he placed a finger under her chin. "You could never hurt me."

Raina's green eyes shimmered.

"I told you, I wasn't leaving you."

"Oh, Devon."

A tear escaped, and he wiped it with his thumb before he pressed his lips to her forehead. She felt so perfect there in his arms, like God made her just for him. The thought settled in Devon, nestling into a deep place in his heart. He loved her.

As his gaze connected with hers again, he longed to

brush his lips across hers. Show her how much he cared for her.

The sound of a male voice clearing nearby stirred him from his longing. He leaned back and slid his hand down her arm, twining his fingers with hers. He kept a loose grasp while his uncle hugged him, followed by his cousins, Rennie and Solana.

As a wave of exhaustion hit him, he whispered to Raina that he needed to sit. She led him to a chair.

"Are you hungry?"

"I could eat."

"I'll fix you a plate."

He continued to hold her hand as she started to walk away. "Raina? Are you alright, sweetheart?"

"Yeah. I'll be right back."

Then she hurried from the table.

Devon sighed. He hoped he would have time to talk to her in private soon. Probably not that day, as he wanted to lie down after eating.

RAINA CHOKED DOWN a sob as she rushed away from Devon. He looked so pale. And he had lost weight. Not that he had much to lose.

After swiping the back of her hand across her cheek, she snagged two plates and made her way through the buffet line, Devon's words ringing in her ears. *I told you I wouldn't leave you.* How could he know she needed to hear exactly those words?

A pang of guilt knifed her. She had no claim to him. He kissed her once. They talked on the phone a few times. Neither declared feelings for the other. She wasn't his girlfriend. Was she?

Once she filled both plates with food, she returned to the

table, placing one in front of him. Then she looked for a seat.

"Raina." Devon patted the empty seat next to him. "No one is brave enough to take your seat."

Heat warmed her cheeks as she slid into it.

"Thanks for fixing me a plate."

His fingers wrapped around hers under the table for the family prayer. He kept it there as he picked at the mac-n-cheese on his plate.

Raina couldn't deny the way he held her hand clarified that she was his girlfriend. She wanted to believe it. But should she?

When she withdrew her hand from his grip, he turned away from his brother mid-sentence. Heat flamed her face.

"What's wrong?" Devon asked.

She tried to laugh it off, as she reached for a knife to cut the chicken breast on her plate.

"Sweetheart."

There was that term of endearment again.

"Tell me."

Raina shook her head and stuffed a bite of chicken in her mouth. He leaned over, sucking in a sharp breath. Great, now she caused him to hurt himself. Probably at his surgery site.

He propped an arm on the back of her chair and whispered to her.

"I missed you. We'll talk soon, okay?"

She sniffed and nodded. He rubbed his hand along the base of her neck. Such a personal, boyfriend-like thing to do. Then he returned to eating his meal.

Raina couldn't explain the storm of emotions inside of her at that moment. Hope that Devon might really care deeply for her. Fear for the same reason. Fear of losing him. Dread over talking about it. Joy that he came home safe. Probably at least ten more feelings mixed with all that.

When she noticed him yawn a second time, she asked if he needed to rest.

"Yeah, I should ask someone to drive me back to my bunk."

"Oh, no, *mijo*. I asked River to make up the guest room for you," Catalina said.

Raina caught the flicker of his frown.

"Mami, I want to sleep in my own bed. I'm well enough to get around on my own."

When his mother started to protest, her husband quietly said her name. She pursed her lips into a thin line. Raina figured it was hard for her to sit by and not help her son. Seemed Catalina tried to remain very involved in her sons' lives.

"I can take you." The words left her mouth before she thought them over.

"That would be nice, but I think Drake is headed over, anyway."

"I still have more work to do here," Drake said, winking at Devon. "You two go ahead."

Raina stood. "Let me clear your plate—"

"Leave them," Drake said. "I'll take care of them."

"Oh. Okay."

Devon stood slowly, placing a hand on his right side. She placed an arm around his waist, hoping he would lean on her. Even though he slung his arm over her shoulders, he put no weight on her as they shuffled out to her car.

"Raina… Thanks for driving me home."

"Sure."

"I… I really enjoyed our phone conversations. And I can't wait to see the work you did at the children's center when I feel a little better."

"Um. Thanks."

She dug her keys out of her purse and pressed the button to disarm her car. Then she held the door open for him.

"Is this too low? I can run back inside to get one of your brothers to—"

"This is fine."

Devon held on to the door as he folded himself onto her low seat. He hissed as he dragged his second leg into the car. Drat. Her car couldn't be good for a man of his height after having his appendix removed. When she reached for the seatbelt, he waved her off.

"I should be fine without it. Unless you're a crazy driver?"

His half smile caused one to stretch across her lips.

"Danica Patrick has nothing on me."

Devon laughed as she eased his door shut. She climbed behind her wheel and started her old car.

After pointing the car toward the bunkhouse, she asked, "Is it okay if I help you in? Do you need to change the bandage or anything?"

"You can come in. I wouldn't object to a little help."

"Oh, but your things. Should I turn around?"

"Raina. Breathe."

"Right."

"We have plenty of gauze and bandages at the bunkhouse. Believe it or not, ranch work can sometimes be dangerous."

She snorted. "Yeah. I guess Adan sliced his arm on something earlier this week. He came into the office and asked Solana to help him. It surprised me she had some surgical glue in the first aid kit in the office."

Devon grinned. "I have a feeling he could have fixed it up at the stables."

"Oh?"

"Tell me you haven't noticed him and Solana staring at each other?"

"I've seen her. Didn't know the feeling was mutual."

"I think they are trying to hide it from each other. Who knows why? Seems silly to deny their feelings..."

Raina wondered why he didn't finish the thought as she parked her car and shut it off. Then she held the car door open for Devon. Getting out appeared more difficult, but he managed. She helped him up the steps and into the bunk-house.

"Kitchen is where we stow the first aid kit."

She looped her arm around his waist and led him to the kitchen. He told her where to find the kit—a box the same size as a portable toolbox. She set it on the table and he dug out the needed supplies. Then he lifted his shirt and slung the waistband of his gym shorts lower. Her breath caught as her face warmed. What had she been thinking, offering to help?

Devon tucked the edge of his shirt under his chin and started peeling back the bandage.

"Here, I can get that," she offered, certain her cheeks might spontaneously combust as hot as they were.

Raina slowly removed the rest of the bandage, rubbing a finger over the skin where the tape had been. When Devon sucked in a sharp breath, she asked if she was hurting him.

"No. Never seen anyone rub behind removing the tape."

"It usually helps with the sting."

"Yeah. It is."

The husky timbre of his voice sent tingles down her spine. She refused to look into his eyes. Instead, she focused on cleaning the incision and bandaging it again. As she secured the last piece of first aid tape, she stepped back.

"There. All better."

Devon dropped his shirt and slid his arm around her waist. Then he scooted out from the table, pulling her onto his lap. She met his gaze and parted her lips. His eyes roamed over her face.

"Thank you," he whispered.

Raina placed her arms behind his neck, feeling the warmth against her forearms. The air sizzled between them and his head angled as he moved closer. She moistened her lips.

"Raina?"

Her eyes flitted shut. "Hmm?"

"Can I kiss you?"

"Please."

Then his lips moved over hers, whisper soft at first. She played with the hair at his nape as he deepened the kiss. When his fingers tangled with her hair, she melted against him. Oh, how special he made her feel. Cherished and loved.

Loved?

Raina tore away, jumping up and taking a step back from the table. Her fingers touched her swollen lips.

A boyish smile stretched across Devon's face as he clasped her other hand, tethering her to him.

"I've been dreaming of that kiss."

His words sent electric waves through her limbs. It was a kiss to dream about. Not that she would vocalize the words. No doubt about it, though. Something had definitely shifted between them. Her fears might warn her off from a relationship with him, but her heart nudged her to ignore those fears.

Raina squared her shoulders, gathering her wits again.

"We best get you settled, mister."

Devon chuckled. "Yes, ma'am."

She helped him back to his bunk and then hurried from the room, lest her heart get any other ideas.

"Raina?"

She paused in the doorway. Devon kissed the tips of two of his fingers and turned them toward her. A grin spread across her face before she ducked out of the bunkhouse.

No matter the surge of emotion whirling inside of her, she was glad Devon made it home safely. And even more glad he kissed her again.

15

TWO DAYS AFTER Devon came home, he crawled out of bed, his mind full of plans. Though he spent a couple of hours with Raina over the last few days, he wanted to do something special for her. He finally felt well enough to drive and only needed a brief nap in the afternoon, like the one he just woke up from.

Glancing at the time on his phone, he smiled. Perfect. Plenty of time to enlist Drake's help to set up a special evening for Raina.

He climbed into his 4Runner, snicking the seatbelt into place. He squirmed until he adjusted it so it didn't cut across the tender spot from his incision. Then he drove over to the dining hall.

When he entered, Drake greeted him.

"Hey, I was wondering if you could help me set up a table in the children's center after Raina leaves for the day."

Drake grinned. "Are you two dating? Officially?"

"I hope to make it official tonight."

"Yes! I knew it."

Devon chuckled. "Glad you're excited about it."

They discussed a menu. Timing. Ambiance. And Drake promised to take care of it.

"I have a new server with some experience at a high end place. I'm sure he'd be happy to take care of you. Name is Mason."

"Do you think Mami would notice if I cut some of her roses?"

"I'll do you one better. I have a few flowers left from the centerpieces we refreshed today. We can make a bouquet out of them. Come on back."

Devon led him to the glass front fridge in the back of the kitchen that served the dining hall. Beautiful carnations, daisies, and some other flowers—he didn't know their names—stood in a vase.

"That looks perfect."

Drake snickered. "I just tossed them in there. But you're right. They look nice as is."

"Alright, I'll take them back with me. Unless you think they'll wilt."

"Naw, you'll be fine."

Drake grabbed a length of clear cellophane, placed the flowers on it, and secured it with a ribbon. Devon marveled at Drake's world. He never realized how artistic his brother could be. Or how much he did in his role as the manager over the dining hall and coffee shop.

"Thanks again, Drake. I know you're busy with all the guests here, too."

Drake squeezed his shoulder. "Anything for my brother. Now *vamos*. I need to check on a few things before we start dinner service."

Devon drove back to the bunkhouse before calling Raina. He supposed he could have stopped in, but he wanted to wait to see the murals until their surprise dinner.

"Hi." A baby screamed in the background and Raina's features twisted. "Just a sec, Dev."

He waited a few minutes before she returned.

"I'm so sorry. I could have called you back. I can't believe you sat here the whole time."

Devon shrugged. "I wasn't in a hurry. Is now a good time?"

Raina shifted the baby to her other hip, stirring a longing

in him. She would be an amazing mother.

"Yeah, I'm good. Unless this little one starts to fuss."

"Can I pick you up at six? For a date?"

"Oh." A smile flitted at the corner of her mouth. "Yeah. Where are we going?"

"It's a surprise."

She frowned. "How am I supposed to know what to wear?"

Devon chuckled. "A summer dress will be fine."

"Dress sandals or wedges?"

"Whatever you want. It's not a fancy place."

"No other hints?"

Before he thought of a snarky answer, the baby let forth a lusty cry, so she hung up. Oh well.

Devon logged onto his laptop to kill some time. Even though the school year started last week, and his doctor recommended at least one more week off work, he looked through the openings for teachers. One piqued his interest until he read the location. Mesa. The opposite end of the Phoenix metro area. A good two and a half hour drive one way, possibly more in traffic.

His shoulders slumped. He really wanted to be a history teacher. But the only school within a reasonable commute was the high school in Wickenburg. And the woman teaching history there had no intention of leaving. At most, he might sub for her when she started her maternity leave, at least that's what the principal said when he called yesterday. She scheduled her leave for February.

Devon folded his hands together and prayed. *Lord, show me what to do. Do I sub this year? Keep looking for something permanent? Give up my dream?*

Subbing would make the most sense to start. There seemed to be a tremendous need. Except it meant he may have to drive for hours if the need was on the east side of the metro area. Maybe longer if it was in the southern suburbs.

Lord, I really want to stay close to Raina. To start building my house and stay on the ranch. I know I said I wanted to leave the ranch, but it's not what I want now. You showed me the importance of family and the unpredictability of life. Thank you for sparing mine. Show me Your will. Amen.

A peace wove through his soul. He didn't have to have all the answers now. He would start with substitute teaching while he continued to pray.

A beep on his phone reminded him he needed to shower before picking up Raina. So he powered off his laptop, stowed it on a shelf, and got ready for his date. This evening was about him and Raina. Not his job.

After he dressed, he sprayed on a little cologne and settled his cowboy hat on his head. He ended up keeping the beard, since Raina said she liked it.

Devon scooped the bouquet off his bed and left the bunkhouse, driving over to Raina's place. He waited a few minutes, praying for their time together. Then he exited his vehicle and knocked on her door.

His cousin opened it.

"Dev, she's still getting ready. Wanna wait in the AC?"

"Thanks Rennie. As long as you don't report me."

She winked. "It's fine. I know the resort manager."

He snorted.

When Raina called his name, Devon turned toward her and swallowed. She looked… Stunning. Sexy. His gaze traveled from her wedge sandals up her shapely legs to the flared skirt of her bright blue sun dress—his favorite color. The dress nipped at the waist and hugged her feminine curves tastefully. At her neck rested a simple gold cross. A pleasant reminder for him to behave himself.

Then his eyes connected with hers. She wore makeup that enhanced her beauty, causing her eyes to stand out even more. His mouth dried up and words disappeared. Remembering the flowers, he angled them toward her. Her fingers brushed his as she accepted them, sending his heart rate racing.

"Oh, they are lovely."

She lowered her head to smell the flowers while maintaining the lock on his gaze. A blush graced the apples of her cheeks. The look did wild things to his insides.

"I'll put them in a vase for you," Rennie volunteered. "Don't want you to be late."

Raina thanked her before taking his outstretched hand. Devon waited until they were alone outside before placing a kiss on her cheek, the sweet fragrance of honey and peaches tickling his nose. He loved the scent that was perfectly Raina.

"You look incredible."

"You look pretty handsome yourself, cowboy. The beard goes nicely with the hat."

Her light laughter warmed his heart.

A few minutes later, he parked by the dining hall.

"Oh. I thought you said it was a surprise."

"Just wait."

Devon rounded his vehicle to help her down. Then he led her to the children's center.

"Devon, where—"

"Patience, sweetheart."

He used his key to unlock the front door. Then he flipped on the lights, jaw slacking at the remodel. He took in the hand-painted characters in an area now dubbed the "Toddler's Cove." Devon clasped her hand and headed toward it as he opened the short door.

"Wow, Raina, I love what you've done with the space." He walked toward the wall and touched the painting of a dog. "You made this?"

"Yeah," she whispered. "I drew everything. Solana and Renata helped me paint it all."

"This is extraordinary. You could illustrate a children's book, with talent like this."

Pink bloomed on her cheeks and Devon pulled her closer, clutching both of her hands in his.

"I'm serious. This is high-quality work."

"Thanks." Her gaze dropped to the floor, pink spreading across her cheeks.

In that moment, Devon realized what a blessing God had given him, rescuing his life in Guatemala. Letting him return home to this beautiful woman who had captured his interest and his heart. Even though she doubted her worthiness and lovability, he couldn't help but fall for her. And he could think of no one more worthy of his love.

Stirring from his musings, Devon placed his hand at the small of Raina's back and escorted her to the table in the corner.

"Oh!"

Her sweet gasp let him know exactly when she noticed the candles casting a soft glow over the white tablecloth. A centerpiece matching the bouquet he gave her sat in the center of the table. Mason held a chair out.

"Miss?"

"Um. Thank you," she replied as she floated onto the seat, smoothing out her skirt.

While Devon took his place across from her, Mason poured a glass of water with lemon for each of them. Raina asked for an orange soda and Devon requested a Coke. After Mason left, Raina turned her gaze on him.

"Devon, what's going on?"

He grinned. Though it might appear foolish, he would start with the question he had been dying to ask her since he first kissed her.

"WILL YOU BE my girlfriend?"

Devon's question wrapped around Raina's heart, making her feel so special—a feeling missing from her life for far too long. She feared trusting him. Did he really want her to be his girlfriend?

"I care about you, Raina. I think I'm falling in love with you and I want to get to know you better."

Raina bit her lower lip. Get to know her. She heard the hint at something longer term in his voice. She closed her eyes. Her secret pressed down on her heart. He would never say such things to her if he knew. And knowing would steal away that soft look in his eyes. She didn't want him to hate her. Or leave her.

But maybe if he really fell in love with her, it would be enough to overlook the endometriosis that robbed her chance for biological children. They could adopt. It didn't mean they couldn't have children at all, right?

Devon dropped his hands in his lap, the tender look fading. No, no, no. She needed his loving gaze to last longer.

"Did I read you wrong? I thought... Do you not have feelings for me?"

She ruined it with her silence. If she wanted to keep him, she had better act fast.

"Devon, I have feelings for you. I..." She looked away as she stuffed her secret deeper. "I am falling for you." Then she allowed her eyes to slide to his.

Devon's cheeks puffed before he blew out a whoosh of air. "Good. So... Will you be my girlfriend?"

"Yes."

A saucy grin tilted up one side of his mouth and he winked at her. Mason returned with the salads and drinks, so they waited for him to leave before Devon prayed.

Even his prayer stirred Raina's heart toward him. He asked God to help them keep their relationship honoring to Him. She knew Devon meant their physical attraction. But the guilt about her secret tried to unearth itself. Raina mentally shoved it away as she joined her boyfriend in a hearty "Amen."

Needing a distraction from the guilt, she asked him about the mission trip. "How was the trip, you know, before the hospital stay?"

"Ha."

He swallowed a bite of salad before telling her about Felipa, Nery, and the boys. "They were so eager to learn about Jesus. It's inspiring. Makes me want to be a better man." He regaled her with a few stories of Felipa the bold before polishing off his salad.

"So you want to go again?"

"Yeah. Raina, you would love it. Maybe not the bugs and jungle. But the kids. Come with me next summer?"

"I'll think about it."

When his shoulders fell, she quickly added, "It's not a brush off, Dev. I will think about it. And pray about it. I want to learn more first. Okay?"

"Yeah. Makes sense."

Silence settled over the room while she chewed her salad. Devon shifted in his chair, and Raina hoped he understood her reasoning. Between bites, she huffed.

"Guess I should have thought about background music," Devon mumbled.

"I have a bluetooth speaker in my office, if you want."

Devon's face lit up. "Yeah, would you mind getting it?"

"Not at all."

When she started to stand, he scooted his chair back and stood to hold her chair. She relished his attentiveness. Once they retrieved the speaker, he set it on a nearby bookshelf.

"What kind of music do you like?"

Raina shrugged. "Most. You pick your favorite."

While he scrolled through an app on his phone, she turned her attention back to her salad. By the time country music love songs flowed through the speakers, Mason returned with their food.

The awkwardness between them grew. It disappointed Raina, as the conversation seemed to flow easily between them when he called her. Why did words seem to flee now?

Raina straightened her back and asked, "Did you ever

learn more about your parents?"

Devon swallowed a bite before responding. "Yeah. Papi said that Devon, Sr. was the middle son. He met Anita at her parents' ranch while they were in high school. Her parents owned an arena where locals practiced for the rodeo. Devon prepared for the pro circuit in team roping."

As they ate, Devon told her about his father's service in the Army and how he died.

"I'm so sorry," Raina said. She knew the pain of losing someone unexpectedly.

"I think once Mami and Papi tell Drake, I'm going to ask them to show us pictures and to share stories with us. They were together for less than ten years. Closer to six, I think. Still, when Mami and Papi answered my questions, it made Devon and Anita feel more real."

Raina glanced away, setting down her silverware. "I wish I had someone to remind me what my parents were like."

"How did they die?"

His caring tone bolstered her courage.

"Do you remember hearing about a shooting at a movie theater about fourteen years ago?"

Devon shook his head.

"Well, they had gone on a date. Left me with a sitter. During the movie, a shooter entered the building and fired into the crowd. Killed my mom instantly. My dad died at the hospital."

She sniffed, trying to keep the sorrow at bay. It had been the first time she talked about it without completely dissolving into hysterics. Maybe God's healing work on her heart had taken root.

Devon reached across the table and held her hand.

"They said they would be back soon. Instead, the sitter stayed overnight with me before calling the cops in the morning to find out what had happened. The next thing I knew, they put me in the foster system, shuffling me from place to place. I lived a chaotic life most days."

"How did you find Jesus?"

Raina snorted. "He found me. Through this older couple I had lived with for a few months. John and Janet Radcliff."

Devon's thumb moved over her hand as Mason entered with a dessert. She waited until he left before she continued.

"They loved me. Bought me new things, like clothes, books, toys. They took me to church."

She coughed, as the memory of being ripped away from them hung heavy over her head. She stumbled through the retelling of that day as Devon listened intently. Good thing their dessert didn't include ice cream, for it would have turned into a puddle.

Then Devon stood and pulled her into his arms, whispering against her hair, "I'm sorry you went through so much heartache."

She snorted. "What doesn't kill you makes you stronger. I think it's something my dad used to say."

Devon rubbed circles on her back. "You are one strong woman, Raina Crawford."

She wrapped her arms around his waist and dropped her head back. "Thanks."

When his gaze turned stormy, she broke the connection. "Let's eat that carrot cake. Did you know it's my favorite?"

"I do now."

He flashed a grin before pressing a kiss to her forehead. Then he took his seat again.

As they finished their dessert, he shared more about his dream of teaching.

"I didn't always want to be a teacher. Then, in the seventh grade, Mr. Seibert gave us a family tree project. We had to interview relatives and include photos from our research. I enjoyed learning about my grandparents and great-grandparents. The rich history behind this place. Padre spent a lot of time helping me with the project, since Papi had been too busy managing the ranch. Mami's parents emigrated from Mexico while she had been a young girl. So on her side of the family, we are first generation Americans. Oh, um…"

Raina finished her last bite of carrot cake. She heard the sadness in his tone.

"I guess Dalton, Dylan, and Derin are. Huh. I don't know about Anita's family. I'll have to ask."

Mason came and cleared the dishes, so Raina propped her elbows on the table and listened while Devon finished his story.

"I loved the project so much and learning about world events in my ancestors' lives that I devoured books about history. Mr. Seibert is the one who planted the seed. My high school history teacher, Mr. Woods, is the one who suggested I could make a career out of my interest in history. He told me how to become a history teacher. After that, I set my course. Taking college classes at night took me a little longer than I would have liked, but I have all the credentials I need."

"But the school year started already," Raina said, wondering if he missed the opportunity to teach this year.

"Teachers leave throughout the year, especially women teachers who decide not to return after having a baby. I have a commitment from the principal at Wickenburg High to teach during his history teacher's maternity leave in February. A minor part of me hopes she stays home after the baby is born."

"What will you do until then?"

"Substitute teach. I could look for something permanent, but if there's even a slight chance they can hire me in Wickenburg, that would be my first choice. I don't want to live far away from you."

Raina's heart softened. She couldn't believe she factored into his decision. She reached over and twined her fingers with his.

"Thank you."

His smile caused warmth to spread through her. Yeah, she was falling for him.

"So, I'll sub this year. Will probably mean some long commutes depending on where the need is—at least until she goes on maternity leave."

When Raina yawned, Devon suggested he take her home, and she agreed. At the door to her home, he spoke sweet words to her softly before gracing her with a brief kiss she would dream about all night.

As she closed the door to her room and readied for bed, guilt pressed in. She still hadn't told him about her secret. She would have to. Soon.

16

As SEPTEMBER ROLLED by, quickly followed by October, Devon thought his life couldn't possibly be better. Subbing gave him the opportunity to use his teaching gift and the flexibility to spend a few days helping Raina at the children's center when more families booked rooms at the resort.

He smiled at her as she rocked his niece Elena back to sleep. He could hardly wait to propose, marry, and start a family together. Raina's motherly instincts fascinated him. She knew just the right words delivered with the perfect tone to calm a frightened child or comfort a clingy toddler. Devon loved watching her interact with kids of all ages.

Thanksgiving was a month away. It would be the perfect time to propose. The entire family thought of Raina as their own. Devon assumed she might enjoy their attention and want him to propose in front of them. He would talk to Mami about it later.

As he gathered the teens and escorted them over to the arena, he thanked God for the beautiful weather and all the blessings He had given. Saving him, healing his body after his appendectomy, nurturing the growing love between him and Raina.

So much had changed in the last five months of his life. After coming to terms with learning the secret about his parents, he lost all desire to leave Vargas Ranch. The place meant so much more to him now.

Though Mami and Papi still dragged their feet—not telling Drake—Devon carved out time with them to learn more about Devon and Anita. He couldn't bring himself to call people he didn't remember his mami and papi. They could never take the place of Catalina and Tres as his heart's parents. Life full of shared laughter and heartaches had made them so.

After dropping the teens at the arena, he meandered along the path back to the children's center, the cool breeze rejuvenating his soul. An idea sparked in Devon's mind. Wouldn't Raina love to know what happened to the Radcliffs? He could find them. See if they remembered her. Maybe reunite them.

She spoke highly of them several times, sharing her desire to create a center or program for middle school foster kids. They could host something like that at the ranch. Perhaps include horses and time at the sports complex. So many opportunities there. He would give it more thought.

When he returned to the children's center, Taylor arrived, so Raina didn't need his help. Devon drove over to the bunkhouse. He retrieved his laptop and set it on the kitchen table. Then he opened his browser and searched for John Radcliff in Omaha. Two phone numbers came back.

He dialed the first one on his phone. It went to voicemail, so he left a message. Then he dialed the second one. After three rings, a man picked up.

"Hello?"

"John Radcliff?"

"Speaking."

"My name is Devon Vargas. I... This will probably sound like an odd question, but did you and your wife foster a little girl named Raina? About fourteen years ago?"

The man coughed. "Is she alright?"

Devon tamped down his excitement. "Yes, sir. She's my girlfriend. Works at the children's daycare center at my family's ranch in Arizona."

"Tell me about her. How is she doing?"

"She speaks fondly of you and Janet."

They talked for a few more minutes. Then Devon set up a time for a video call Friday evening, so John could speak with Raina.

"You must care for her a great deal," John said. "To go to the trouble of tracking me down."

"I love her." He kept to himself his desire to marry her.

After they ended the call, Devon drove to town to look at engagement rings. He walked through several stores before returning to the first. They had the perfect one, so he purchased it and a gold heart-shaped necklace. He would give that to her on Friday, saving the engagement ring for Thanksgiving.

Yeah, God had blessed him tremendously. He shared his gratitude in a prayer before driving back to the ranch.

"I HAVE A surprise for you," Devon said.

Raina's pulse ticked up.

"Let's drive out to the sunset overlook."

"It won't set for a few hours yet," she reminded him.

"Not to worry. We'll have a picnic supper and I have a surprise."

"That's not the surprise?"

Devon grinned. "Nope. Come on."

When he caught her hand and led her to the truck, she giggled.

"In a hurry?"

"Yeah. Just want to make sure we have time to settle in."

Raina smiled as she climbed into the passenger seat. Devon might be acting weird, but she had grown to love his surprises. Never disappointed her once. She trusted him fully.

Fully? That couldn't be completely true. Otherwise, she wouldn't keep dodging his questions about how many kids she wanted. And she would have told him the truth. Ugh. Now certainly didn't feel like the right time.

Burying those concerns, she pressed the button to lower the window, allowing the cool evening air in. She loved Arizona. The hot summer seemed to drag on, but late October brought pleasant temperatures, especially in the mornings and evenings.

After a few minutes, they arrived at the lookout spot. Devon held her door. She asked how she could help, so he handed her a blanket. She spread it out and sat down. When he set his laptop on top of the picnic basket, her curiosity grew.

"What's this about?"

"Just a few more minutes."

Devon tapped on his phone, creating a hotspot. Then he connected his laptop to it and opened video conferencing. He started a meeting. So odd.

"Devon—"

The man's face on the screen before her caused an abrupt end to her words. Though silver hair graced his head, she would recognize John Radcliff anywhere. Tiny wrinkles surrounded those kind, dark eyes. No face had ever made her feel so safe. Her throat constricted as Devon greeted him. The sight of the man who had been like a father to her sent waves of joy and sorrow through her simultaneously. She tried to speak, but she struggled to find her voice. Devon continued the friendly conversation, unaware of her internal battle.

"Raina." John held a fist to his mouth and coughed. "It's so good to see you."

Her lower lip trembled. "John."

Devon rubbed a hand over her back before he looped his arm behind her. She found comfort in the gentle warmth radiating from him.

"How have you been?" John asked.

Then the words loosened. She told him about the scholarship and college, skipping the dark years she spent in the foster system.

"I drove to Arizona by myself. It was a little scary to sleep in my car, but I knew this job was perfect." She craned her neck to look at Devon. "I thought I lost it before the interview, having accidentally dumped my lunch on him."

John and Devon both chuckled. As their laughter faded, Raina worked up the courage to ask the questions she had held back.

"Where's Janet?"

John's face screwed up, clearly pained by it.

"I'm sorry. You don't have to tell me."

"Raina, I'm the one that is sorry. She passed a few months after... They took you away."

"No." The sob lodged in her throat, causing a dreadful sound to escape while tears brimmed.

"Oh, honey. We wanted to adopt you. Had asked about it. I tried to push for it even after learning about Janet's cancer. The social worker wouldn't listen to reason. She said I couldn't possibly care for a dying spouse and a little girl. Janet's heart broke. She made me promise to find you and make the adoption happen."

The camera jittered as John shifted in his seat. Raina's heart ached. They had wanted her to be their daughter.

"I pestered that social worker for months after you left. I sought legal action, and the court denied me. No one wanted a widower grieving for his wife to raise a girl on his own. It made no sense to me. How many single dads raise their daughters every day in this country? But a man wants to adopt a child that he loves like the daughter he never had and it's not possible?"

Raina regained control of her emotions. He needed to hear her heart on this.

"John, I did not know. I loved you and Janet and prayed for years that you would find me and take me home. I wanted you to be my parents. I can't believe they kept us apart."

John's voice cracked when he spoke. "I never stopped praying for you, honey. You are my heart's daughter. Even though I haven't laid eyes on you for fourteen years, I love you more today than I did the few months you lived with us. I know it would have thrilled Janet to see us reunited."

They talked for another thirty minutes, catching up on life. She learned John had remarried and lost his second wife last year. Such great losses. He had turned seventy-five last year and his doctor recommended he move to a warmer climate.

"You should come visit, John," Devon said. "As a guest of my family."

When John hesitated, Raina turned toward Devon. "Please," she pleaded with her boyfriend.

"Come for Thanksgiving. If money is a concern, I'm happy to help."

"No. That's not it. I just can't... You really want to see me, Raina?"

"Yes! More than anything."

"Then I'll come."

After they signed off, she gripped Devon in a fierce embrace.

"Thank you, Dev. That's got to be the best thing anyone has ever done for me."

"You're very welcome. I have one more surprise for you."

When he reached into his pocket and pulled out a jewelry box, her heart squeezed tight. After everything he had done for her, she would have to tell him she couldn't bear his children. It would ruin the perfect evening and best day of her life.

"I thought you might like to remember this day, so I

bought you this."

He opened the box to reveal a lovely heart-shaped neck-lace. Raina breathed easier. She could keep her secret a little longer. But she really must tell him soon. It wasn't fair to him to hold on to it.

"It's beautiful. Thank you Devon. For everything. For finding John and the call and this."

"I would do anything for you, Raina. I love you."

She placed her hand on his bearded cheek as she guided his lips to hers. "I love you, too, Devon."

Maybe love could conquer the hurt he would feel when she gave him the shattering news. It just wouldn't be to-night.

17

THE DAY BEFORE Thanksgiving, Devon grew nervous. Probably for no reason. Raina would say yes, he was sure of it. Yet, he couldn't shake the sense of foreboding as he left to pick up John Radcliff from the airport.

The resort was filled to capacity, mostly families, so Raina couldn't go with him. They needed her on site. She planned to have John over at her place for supper. Both Rennie and Solana promised to make themselves scarce for the evening. Devon smiled as he remembered how worried she had been that he would be upset she excluded him from the meal. He hadn't minded. It was a private reunion. They agreed Devon would stop by for dessert at seven before driving John back to his parents' house. Since there were no available rooms at the resort, Mami had insisted John stay with them, instead of booking a room in town.

Devon scanned the crowd for John Radcliff. When he spotted him, he waved. The man seemed older in person, walking slower and balancing with a cane.

"Welcome, John," Devon said before hugging him.

"Good to meet you in person."

"I can grab your luggage for you if you want to find a seat." As he said the words, Devon realized there were only a handful of seats in the baggage claim area. Looked like they were already taken.

"I'll be fine." John chuckled. "You're a lot taller than I

pictured."

Devon smiled. "Yeah. I'm the tallest of my brothers."

For the first time since learning about his birth parents, he didn't stumble over the word "brothers." Things seemed to return to normal for him. Good. He would be in a solid place to help Drake deal with it. Mami said they planned to wait until after the holidays to tell him. Devon thought they should have told Drake months ago, but he kept that to himself. It would all come out in God's timing, anyway.

"There it is!"

John's voice drew him from his thoughts.

"Which one?"

"The black one."

Devon noticed four black ones in a row.

"It just turned the corner."

Devon sprinted toward it, grabbing it off the belt. He looked at the name tag. Since it belonged to John, he wheeled it toward the older man.

"Anything else?"

"That's it."

Devon led him to the short-term parking. Once they found his vehicle, he stowed the bag in the trunk and John's cane behind his seat.

When he merged onto the highway out of the Phoenix metro area, Devon braved the question on his mind.

"I was wondering, sir, if I could have your blessing for Raina's hand. I figure you're the closest relationship she has to a father."

John chuckled. "Devon, I think I'm more of her grand-father's age than a father. Just turned seventy-five this year. Come to think of it, that might have played a part in the court's decision. I had been sixty-one back then."

"She speaks of you like a fatherly influence."

"Well, for what it's worth, if you love her and she loves you, then I'll be happy to bless it, even though it's not my right."

"I respectfully disagree, sir. I think it will please Raina to know you bless our relationship."

"Then consider yourselves blessed."

RAINA GLANCED AT the clock for the third time. She really needed to head home and put dinner on.

"Go. We've got this," Taylor said. "Get ready to spend time with your dad."

Raina's face heated. "Are you sure?"

"Go." Josh and Amber echoed.

"Solana said she'd help us close up if we need anything," Amber added.

"Okay. Thanks."

She retrieved her purse and travel mug before rushing out the door. It only took a minute to drive to her home.

The word curled around her heart. In the five months since she arrived at Vargas Guest Ranch & Resort, the place truly felt like home in a way no other place ever had. Maybe the Radcliff's. She started her career here. Fell in love with Devon. Grew through her sorrow. Been adopted by Catalina and Tres and Devon's extended family.

Family dinner with the Vargases had become the highlight of her week. They treated her with kindness and made her feel like she truly belonged.

Now she and John Radcliff had been reunited. He was a man she thought of as a father. She cherished their twice weekly calls since Devon reintroduced them. He even mentioned looking for a house in the area while visiting. Raina prayed he might move to Arizona. It would be nice to have him nearby.

When she entered her home, Renata greeted her. "I'll be out of your way in a minute. Just baked these cookies for you."

"Aw, thanks."

That was just like Renata. She loved doing homey things like that. It eased Raina's anxiety since she wasn't the best baker.

Renata hugged her and prayed with her before taking off.

Raina paused, breathing deeply and letting it out slowly, savoring the peace before turning her attention to preparing a salad. She grilled some chicken and then cut it up, mixing it with Alfredo sauce. Then she started the water to boil fettucini.

A knock sounded at the door. Wiping her hands on a towel, she headed toward it. She set the towel on the back of a chair. A hand shot to her hair. Not that she could do anything about her curly mane. Then she opened the door.

A grin spread across John Radcliff's face.

"John, welcome to my home."

He stepped inside. Raina glanced toward Devon's vehicle. He waved before backing out. Then she closed the door.

"Dinner's almost ready."

"Time for a hug, honey?"

"Of course."

John's embrace filled every longing for a father's affection in her life. The water hissed from the stove as drops sprayed onto the burner, cutting the hug short.

"Would you mind pouring some drinks while I finish up?"

"Sure thing."

"I'll take an orange soda."

John chuckled. "Still like that nasty stuff?"

Raina giggled. "Yeah."

He poured himself a glass of water and set both on the table.

"Please have a seat," Raina said.

She grabbed the salads from the fridge and set a bowl out for each of them. Then she drained the pasta and dumped it into a serving bowl before topping it with the chicken and Alfredo. She placed it on the table with serving utensils. Then she eased into the chair next to John.

"Shall I pray?" he asked.

Raina nodded, as memories of his deep voice and impassioned prayers resurfaced. She hadn't realized how much of those few months she had carried with her all these years. When he finished the prayer, she whispered one of gratitude in her heart.

"You look good, Raina. Janet would be so proud of you."

She swallowed a bite of salad. "That means so much to me."

"That young man of yours loves you."

"I know. I love him too. Except..."

John gave her his full attention. "Except?"

"I have a condition that... I can't have kids. And I haven't told him yet."

"Why not?"

Raina's stomach knotted. "I'm afraid he'll leave me if he knows the truth. I... I can't lose him, John."

"Hmm. Seems to me like you need to tell him."

"He wants kids. I know it. So do I. But he won't be satisfied with someone who can't give him a child."

"How can you know that? You said yourself you haven't told him."

"I know him. It's very important to him."

"Maybe you should tell him and trust God with the outcome."

Raina served a portion of the pasta dish onto her plate. "I'll think about it."

The conversation shifted away from that uncomfortable subject. John shared more about Janet's cancer and all he went through in those days.

"I still wanted you, Raina. I fought hard to adopt you."

"I know you did all you could. I'm just glad we can be...

Family? Can I call you my family?"

"I'd love nothing more, honey."

Her phone buzzed. Devon asked if she still wanted him over for dessert. She texted back he could come over. He let himself in when he arrived.

She started the dishwasher, then set out napkins and the plate of cookies.

"Renata baked these for us."

Devon waggled his eyebrows. "You don't bake?"

"Not really."

"It's alright. There are plenty of people on the ranch that can."

Raina smiled at his teasing.

As John and Devon got to know each other better, she interjected periodically, content to watch them. John was a kind soul. The years had not exaggerated that memory of him. And she could tell from every glance, he loved her like a daughter.

Thank you, Lord, for bringing him back into my life. Bless us with many more years to come.

18

THANKSGIVING DAY AT last.

Devon looked around his bunk, patted his pocket, and let out a sigh of relief. The ring box left a bulge, so he removed the ring from the box, tossing the box in the console of his vehicle. Then he tucked the ring in his pocket.

Today was the day he would propose to Raina. Sweat beaded on his forehead, causing him to roll down the window for relief. The cool breeze soothed his skin. She would say yes. He had nothing to worry about. He had prayed long and hard over this decision, always arriving at a sense of peace.

Though he had wanted to pick her up and drive over to the ranch house together, Raina left early with Renata to help in the kitchen. He spotted Rennie's Jeep as he parked. He loved how seemless Raina fit into his family. Mami loved her and that was important to him.

When he entered the house, John and Padre greeted him first.

"They wouldn't let us old timers help," John said. "So we're trading life stories."

"I like this one," Padre said, hooking his thumb toward John.

Devon figured they were around eight years apart in age, so no surprise, they hit it off.

"Your gal is in the kitchen," John said.

"Enter at your own risk."

Devon laughed, knowing the women rarely appreciated the men breaking into their girl time. Still, he entered the kitchen, eager to see Raina.

"*Mijo!*"

Mami spotted him first. "Say your greetings, then *vamos.*"

"Si, Mami."

He bent down, placing a kiss on her cheek. She winked at him, softening her earlier warning.

Devon made his way over to Raina, who appeared to be mixing up the stuffing. Despite Mami's Hispanic heritage, she humored Papi with a few traditional dishes. He strode toward Raina. Then he wrapped his arms around her waist and dropped a few kisses along her neck.

"Devon!"

Then he spun her around, brushing his lips across hers for a few seconds.

"New love," Madison grumbled.

"You're just annoyed because the baby keeps kicking you in the ribs," River teased. "I think it's sweet."

Brisa sat at the kitchen table, nursing her newborn. "Says the romance writer."

"Hey, love is my business. Literally."

"Cuz, you better leave while you can," Solana teased him. "Dalton is outside checking on the turkeys."

"Hey, my husband resembles that remark," Madison teased.

Devon whispered in Raina's ear. "Talk to you later. Have fun."

Then he headed out to the back patio, still smiling over his sisters-in-law's banter. They had welcomed Raina into their fold and it pleased him.

He caught up with his brothers while the turkeys finished cooking. Then he helped Dalton carry them inside for carving. Papi and Derin—shock of all shocks—carved the turkeys. Derin claimed at least one of them ought to learn how to serve the birds properly. That brought a snicker from Drake, who probably knew how to carve a turkey, given his work in the dining hall.

Devon studied the growing crowd. His brothers and their wives, except the single Drake. His parents. Uncle Diego, Aunt Katie, and his cousins. Harley and Heidi Franco, Dylan's in-laws, and his best friend Adan — still single. Devon's nieces and nephews. Padre. John Radcliff. Each year, the gathering multiplied.

Would he and Raina be married by this time next year? He did not know if she wanted a long engagement or not. He would be satisfied with whatever made her happy.

The aroma of smoked turkey filled the room, mingling with the traditional scent of sage, onion, and garlic coming from the stuffing. His stomach growled as the last dish landed on the table with a soft plunk.

He bowed his head, reaching for Raina's hand. She curled her fingers around his. Their first Thanksgiving together. At the end of Papi's prayer, they all sat. He held a chair for Raina before taking his own.

As the time to propose grew closer, the more nervous Devon became. He ate less than most years. Thankfully, no one seemed to notice.

Once the dishes and kitchen were cleaned up, the family gathered in the great room.

Devon cleared his throat, reaching for Raina's hand. He could do this.

WHAT A WONDERFUL day! Raina's heart filled nearly to overflowing as she followed Devon into the great room. She was glad she had helped prepare the meal. She learned so much about River, Brisa, and Madison during that time.

They were wonderful women she gladly called friends.

How far she had come since arriving at the ranch. So many amazing friendships. Her life seemed empty before. Now all she had to do was look around the room and joy filled her soul.

As Devon's gentle grip enclosed her hand, the sound of his throat clearing broke into the silence. All eyes turned towards her as his voice echoed in the room, causing her breath to hitch in her chest.

"Raina, I couldn't think of a better day for this. I think you know how much I love you, but I want to say it again. I love you, Raina Crawford."

No, no, no. He hadn't hinted at a thing. As much as she longed for a lifetime with him, this couldn't happen now. She thought she had more time before she must reveal her secret.

Raina's heart pounded in her chest, matching the intensity of the emotions swirling inside her. The day had begun with such promise, filled with laughter and joy. But now, as she stood there with her throat constricted and her body trembling, she couldn't help but feel the weight of impending tragedy.

Devon dropped to one knee, still holding her hand. He dug into his pocket with his other hand, producing a sparkly diamond ring.

Her gaze tore from him, traveling the room. The Vargas women collectively gasped as excitement brightened their expressions. She couldn't believe this was happening now. Her time was up. She had to tell him. Her failure to do so before now meant she had to tell him in front of his entire family and hers. It would crush him. He would never forgive her for this.

Closing her eyes tightly, Raina tried to steady her breathing, hoping to find some semblance of composure. But the tears welled up, threatening to spill over and betray her fragile state. How had it come to this? How could something so wonderful turn into something so devastating?

"Would you do me the honor of becoming my wife?"

The delicious turkey sat on her stomach like a boulder. Bile threatened to crawl up her throat.

Like ripping off a band-aid, the truth shot from her mouth. There was no way Devon Vargas would want her now.

19

"I CAN'T HAVE children."

Devon cocked his head to the side, confused by Raina's words. They made no sense. She was supposed to say yes. Or squeal and jump up and down. Or toss some witty reply. It didn't matter what or how. It was supposed to be an affirmation of her love for him and her desire to spend her life with him.

Instead, she repeated the baffling words twice more.

"Devon, I can't have children."

Mami's muttered words in Spanish echoed the shock in his own heart.

"What?"

His breath grew shallow as the numbness continued to tighten its grip around his heart. With each passing moment, his vision narrowed, the world around him fading into a blurry haze. The weight on his chest became almost suffocating. What was Raina saying?

"Please, stand up. This is... Hard enough."

The coolness of the tile floor seeped through his jeans, reminding him he still kneeled in front of the woman he loved. The woman who had not said yes. Instead, she spewed an awful soul-crushing string of words at him.

"I have endometriosis. The doctors said the scarring in my uterus is too severe. I won't be able to become pregnant."

Devon shot to his feet, scowling. His hand shook as he tried to stuff the ring back inside his pocket.

"Are you saying you won't marry me? If you don't love me, then just say so. Don't make up lies."

"It's not a lie. No matter how much I wish it weren't true, I will always be barren."

Numbness wrapped around his heart, squeezing out the life, love, and joy that should have cemented this moment in his memory forever. As her sobs knifed through him, rage coursed through his veins. How could she have lied to him? All this time, he thought she knew he wanted kids. Kids with his bloodline. Kids to preserve Devon and Anita's legacy.

"How could you do this, Raina? You know Drake and I are the last of our line. That our parents died when I was little and when Drake was born. I have to have kids. Kids with my DNA!"

Redness tinged her eyes, making the green he loved so much pop even brighter. Instinct propelled him to hold her, but he forced it back. He would not comfort this woman. She betrayed him. Let him believe she loved him.

"I love you, Devon. We could adopt."

Devon growled, spinning away from her. As he showed her his back, he stormed out of the house. He was done with her. Done with her lies. Though it tore his heart to pieces, he had to walk away. Move on.

Didn't she understand?

He slammed his 4Runner's door closed, causing it to rock sharply to one side before settling. Smashing the start button, the engine growled to life, more vibrantly than his foul mood tolerated. He jerked the shifter into Reverse, spinning the wheels on the gravel lot. Then he jammed it into Drive.

It was up to him to carry on his family line. It meant the world to him. She had to have known that. How could she hide the truth? For so long. How could she lead him on?

He drove toward his lookout spot — the place he went to think through the most difficult of life's challenges. It should have soothed him like it usually did, except shared memories with Raina filled his mind. Their steak dinner in the car after he comforted her from her childhood pain. The dozens of times they watched the sunset and the moon rise. The first video call with John Radcliff. She had become engrained in his life, his heart.

Maybe he should take that teaching job in Mesa. Move there. It was still open. And he couldn't stomach living so close to her. Not anymore.

RAINA COULDN'T STOP shaking. Devon's rejection hurt worse than any loss she had experienced prior to that moment. She would love to spend the rest of her life as his wife. But their relationship had been doomed to fail from the beginning.

"I have to have kids. Kids with my DNA!"

The words rang in her ears and the darkness in his eyes flashed repeatedly in her mind's eye. There was no hope for them. Not now. She betrayed him and he would never forgive her for it. She knew it.

As she swayed, John came alongside her. "Let's go outside and talk, honey."

Her feet shuffled as the father of her heart led her onto the patio. The patio where she first told Devon she was an orphan. She couldn't look at the place where he found her that day. Everything hurt too much. His rejection ripped her heart from her chest, leaving behind an empty, lifeless shell.

"Here, sit."

John helped her to a cushioned chair. Then he scooted another to face her before easing into it.

"Raina, it's not over. You two love each other too much.

There are many options for having children. It doesn't have to be the end of your relationship."

"He'll never forgive me."

"Well, I'll be praying you're wrong and that God will soften his heart."

John held her hands in his gnarled ones. "Though Invitro probably won't work in your case, you can search for a surrogate if Devon pushes for a biological child between the two of you."

Raina wiped the tears from her cheeks. "How do you know so much about it?"

"Janet had the same condition."

Raina sat up straighter. Had God brought her family who understood her health issue?

"We decided not to pursue it when we were younger, but we researched it and even interviewed surrogates. Through prayer, we felt God called us to foster instead."

Raina frowned at him. "But you were older when I came to live with you."

"Yes, we were. We had fostered dozens of kids when we were in our thirties and forties. We were still in the computer system when you lost your parents. The social worker remembered us, though we had fostered no one for a decade. She thought you would do well under our care."

The faint smell of hickory smoke lingered in the air from the earlier smoking of the Thanksgiving turkeys. The bright sun cast shadows against the mountain behind John. Raina allowed his words to sink in at last.

"What do I do?"

"Give him some time. He'll come around, honey. He loves you and I still believe love, grounded in a man of God, will conquer all. Even this."

She hoped so. Because if it didn't, she wasn't sure she could stay at the place that had become home to her. It would be too painful to see him all the time or to run into his family.

DRAKE VARGAS BLINKED. His parents weren't really his parents. His brothers weren't really his brothers. Except Devon.

His vision narrowed as his airways constricted. He patted his pockets. Drat. Forgot his inhaler. Didn't expect to need it on Thanksgiving Day.

Dizziness washed over him as he sank onto the nearest couch. Somehow, the aroma of smoked turkey and stuffing registered in his mind, despite the lack of oxygen in his lungs.

"Inhaler!" Mami's frantic voice sounded far away. "Here, *mijo*."

She pressed it into his hand and helped him sit up straighter. She must still keep one on hand for emergencies. He puffed the medicine into his lungs, closing his eyes. He tried to breathe deeply, but the air didn't fill his lungs as fully as he needed. A second breath. A third.

"How many more family secrets are there?" Derin shouted. "Come on, Madi. We're leaving!"

"No more," Padre muttered next to him.

"*Mijo!*" Mami's voice shouted after his older brother. Nope. Not his brother.

The sound of Derin's dually roared to life in the distance as Drake's vision cleared. Lots of crying and yelling echoed throughout the great room. Drake couldn't make out all the conversations over the words ringing in his ears. The twins erupted with their toddler cries, followed by Dylan's newborn.

He loved those kids. Wanted to be their uncle. But they weren't really his nieces and nephew.

The thought tightened his chest again and constricted his throat.

Devon claimed their parents—Devon and Drake's—had died. That meant Mami and Papi weren't really his parents? But...

He searched the far recesses of his memory for anything that would lead him to believe they weren't.

"Breathe, Drake." Papi's voice.

"Does he need a second dose? Hospital?" River asked as Dalton swooped in to claim the twins. He strode out of the room. Probably taking them to their cribs.

Work-roughened hands laid across Drake's cheeks, turning his face towards Papi's.

"Drake. Breathe. Now!"

He forced himself to try, studying the older man's face. Blue eyes widened. He must look a fright.

"Again!"

Again, Drake tried to suck in gulps of air.

Finally, the wheezing stopped. His airways cleared. Oxygen made its way into his bloodstream. It was the worst asthma attack he had had in years.

Raina sobbed nearby, crumpling to the floor. Devon shot to his feet. Leaving his almost fiancée behind, his brother tore from the house.

Drake felt numb as Devon's words replayed over and over, like severe buffering from an online video streaming service. It kept jumping back to the same place, never advancing to the next scene.

His breathing may have returned to normal, but nothing about his life would ever be the same again. His parents weren't his parents.

And they had lied.

And Devon had known and said nothing to him.

Even Raina knew. How did she know? How could Devon tell her and not him? His brother? His only true blood brother?!

He had to get out of there. Flee. Get space to think.

Papi's face came into view and Drake pushed away from

him, jumping to his feet.

"How could you lie to me?"

Then his legs ate up the distance to the front door, his mother's—no, not his mother—wails growing louder behind him. He slammed the heavy door shut, causing the glass inlay to rattle. Then he hopped on his bike and cranked the engine. It growled, an angry sound matching the anger reverberating through Drake's soul.

His entire life had been a lie. He would trust none of them ever again.

20

SUNDAY AFTERNOON, DEVON met Greg at *The Lariat* for lunch. Yeah, he was avoiding both Raina and his family. He had to skip family dinner. Couldn't handle the looks from his family. Or the questions. Or face the possibility of running into Raina. So, when Greg texted him for a time to get together, he suggested lunch on Sunday.

Devon huffed as he parked on the side street next to the café. He scuffed his booted feet along the sidewalk as he ambled toward the door. Greg reached it at the same time. He man-hugged his friend before holding the door open.

When he entered the bistro, he immediately noticed a different picture hanging where his used to. He hadn't been in for months, so he wondered when it sold. He took a seat in the booth across from Greg, not bothering with the menu. He knew what he wanted.

"How was the proposal? Did she like it? When is the wedding date?" Greg's cheerful expression cut through Devon. Guess he forgot to tell him.

"We broke up."

"What?! What happened?"

Devon slumped. "She can't have kids."

"So?" Greg's lip turned up in disgust.

Devon frowned. "So. I told you about my parents."

"And?"

"I have to have kids, Greg. Kids of my own."

Greg slapped the menu down hard on the table. "You know, for a smart cowboy, you're acting awfully stupid right now."

Devon narrowed his eyes.

"You obviously love her. And she loves you. Having biological kids is a deal breaker? Really? I thought you weren't so shallow."

"Look, if you're just gonna insult me, I can go." He started to slide out of the booth.

Greg ran a hand through his hair. "I'm sorry. You surprised me, is all. Sit. I'll leave off."

Devon scooted to the center of the bench, thankful the server delivered their drinks. Sipping his soda gave him a chance to cool off.

"I hope my news doesn't bother you."

"Tell me," Devon encouraged his friend, letting go of his frustration.

"Caitlyn and I are getting married. We're moving to Guatemala."

"Really?"

"Yeah. She quit her day job and joined up with the mission. We're raising support. And we both feel God is calling us to serve down there. At least for a few years, until we have kids. Maybe longer, if it's God's plan."

Devon mentally shook off his earlier anger. "Wow. That's amazing. How can I help?"

"There's my friend."

Devon rolled his eyes.

"I'll send you a link if you and your family want to help sponsor us."

"Of course."

"And you can come back next summer."

"Planning on it."

Greg expelled a loud breath as the server delivered their food.

"I was hoping you had better news for me this morning."

"Why?" Devon asked.

"'Cause Felipa's uncle passed. She's living at the or-phanage full time now. She asks about you all the time."

Devon's heart melted. He wished he could help her.

"I was gonna suggest that you and Raina consider adopting her."

"Greg—"

"I know. Not possible now. International adoptions are hard enough and take long enough with two qualified par-ents. A single dad? That won't happen."

Devon sighed. He wished he could be that for Felipa. But it wasn't possible. Who knew how long it would take him to find a wife, much less get over Raina? Felipa needed a papi now.

"Oh well. God will provide," Greg muttered before bit-ing off a chunk of his sandwich.

Greg's words hounded him well into the evening. Dev-on tossed and turned all night, heart heavy about Raina. About Felipa.

Had his rejection of Raina really been that shallow? He wanted kids of his own. Sure, he was open to adop-tion—especially if it was Felipa. But was it so wrong to want to have kids with his DNA? Especially after losing his birth parents?

Yeah, it was thinking like his that could have kept Raina from being adopted.

The thought seared his soul. Just how important was his desire? Had he been too harsh? Should he have talked to her instead?

That really uncomfortable feeling in his chest plagued him for a solid week after the conversation with Greg. Con-viction. He knew that's what it was. He had been very wrong to break up with Raina over her health.

Lord, forgive me.

He knew Raina's forgiveness was what he needed. He

had to repair his relationship with her. Love for her welled up in him. He had been so very wrong. Now he had to figure out how to make it right.

THE SECOND MONDAY after Thanksgiving. Christmas was in full swing at Vargas Ranch. The day after Thanksgiving, everyone pitched in to turn the resort into a Christmas wonderland. But Raina's heart hadn't been in it. The decorations mocked her. Any cheeriness vanished when Devon walked out on her. She blinked back tears, straightening her shoulders.

After logging into her computer, she double checked the list of food allergies for the kids. The team diligently documented them, as per usual. The text to the chef would fire off in another half-hour. She had nothing to worry about, at least not at work.

John came by last night to check on her. He said that Dylan Vargas's wife owned a house in the nearby hamlet of Forepaugh. Her renters moved out a few months ago, so they offered it to him. He had signed the rental agreement that day. They had converted it for Braden's disability years ago. John liked the ramp at the entrance. It made walking up the porch easier with his knee replacement.

Then he surprised her by asking if she wanted to move into one of the other bedrooms. She promised to pray about it. As she did this morning, the idea grew on her. She could help him with cooking and cleaning. John tried to act like he could handle it all, but she had her doubts. His mobility seemed to change with the wind. Good one day, struggling the next. If she moved in, they could get to know each other even better and she could help with some of the daily chores, easing his burden.

"Hey."

Raina's back stiffened at the sound of Devon's voice from the doorway to the resort office. Hurt rolled over her, raw and fierce, as she swiveled her chair to meet his gaze.

He looked amazing—handsome and perfect—as he braced his shoulder against the doorway. His dark brown cowboy hat shaded his green eyes. The snap front western shirt stretched over his chest, tucked neatly into faded denim. A brown belt with a simple silver buckle circled his waist. One leg crossed over the other.

She missed him.

"Can we talk?"

Against her will, Raina nodded her head, her heart winning over her pain.

"Can you break away for an hour?"

Raina sighed heavily. "Sure."

After she let Amber know, she followed Devon out to his 4Runner. She sat in the awkward silence as he drove to their lookout spot. Hope sprang out of the freshly tilled soil of her heart.

Devon parked and retrieved two folding camp chairs from his trunk as Raina slid down from the passenger seat. He motioned for her to sit before he took the chair next to hers.

Staring out over the pinks, tans, and yellows of the winter desert below, she breathed in the cool air, allowing it to fill her lungs and restore her soul. Cattle dotted the pasture in the valley below. Both of them sat in stillness, soaking up the natural beauty for several minutes.

"Raina." Devon's voice sounded as rusty as an old door hinge. He cleared his throat before he continued. "I have wronged you. Most likely wounded you so deeply, you may never forgive me."

What was he saying? She had wronged him by not telling him her secret long ago.

When the warmth of his hand covered hers, she allowed it, growing more hopeful by the second.

"I should not have walked out on you. Or given you the silent treatment these past few days. I've been a shallow, selfish fool who doesn't deserve your love."

Now she angled toward him, desperate to see his face. His gaze met hers.

"We can adopt. Look for a surrogate. Or foster. Or learn to accept life as a childless couple. None of those things are more important than you and I'm so very sorry for ever causing you to believe that for even a minute."

A tear trickled down her cheek. He said she was more important than having kids. She was not trash.

"Can you forgive me?"

The sorrow and sincerity in his green eyes unleashed the tears in full force. She bit her lower lip and nodded until she recovered.

"Yes, Devon. Can you forgive me?"

"Already have."

Raina moved off her chair and sat on Devon's lap, wrapping her arms behind his neck. Then she pressed her lips to his, their salty tears merging as the healing work of forgiveness bonded their hearts together again.

The chair groaned and creaked right before the sound of splintering plastic echoed through the air. Devon let out an "oof" as the chair gave way, his arms securing her against his strength—a promise of the forever they would share. Their laughter rang loud and clear over the valley below.

"Raina?"

"Yeah."

"Will you marry me?"

"Yes."

Then Devon scooted her to the side before presenting her with the sparkly diamond ring. He slid it onto her finger before he sealed the promise with a soul-deep kiss. Raina thanked God for bringing her to Vargas Ranch and for her smart cowboy before returning her fiancé's kiss.

Epilogue

———

July (seven months later)

"ARE YOU READY?"

Raina twisted her hands together over her husband's question. Her chest tightened in anticipation. The crowded bus bounced over deep ruts in the mountain road, causing her to slam into his side. When she tried to scoot over, his arm held her close.

"We're almost there."

"Why did I let you talk me into *this* for a honeymoon?"

Devon's grin warmed her insides. She hoped that feeling would never fade.

"Because you love kids as much as I do. It's perfectly us."

The deep groaning of the diesel engine cut off anything else he may have said as the driver downshifted. The last stretch of the dirt road steepened. She held her breath as it came into view.

"Oh, it's beautiful!"

"No one has called it that before," Greg muttered from the seat across the aisle.

"Hon, no one has made the journey to meet their daughter here before," Caitlyn said as she nudged her husband's arm. "And it is beautiful, in a rustic, jungle charming sort of way."

Devon and Greg burst out laughing. Raina ignored them. It was beautiful to her for exactly the reason Caitlyn mentioned.

After seven months of planning, learning Spanish, meetings with attorneys, and sporadic video calls, Raina and Devon had finally arrived in Guatemala moments away from meeting the daughter of her heart. Tears pooled in her eyes, blurring her vision. The entire experience felt surreal.

"Hey. It will be alright," Devon said, massaging the base of her neck, a habit she enjoyed whenever her emotions overwhelmed her.

"I'm just so happy, Dev."

His warm lips brushed her forehead. "Me, too, sweetheart."

The bus jerked to an abrupt stop. The doors squeaked loudly as they swung open, letting her daughter's delighted chatter filter in. Raina bolted to her feet and rushed down the aisle, unable to wait one minute longer, hips bumping against the back of each seat.

As she stepped off the bus, the thick, humid air slammed against her face. Bugs nipped her skin but her focus narrowed as she called out, "Felipa!"

The most beautiful girl she had ever seen flashed the brightest smile right before she launched herself into Raina's arms. She hugged her close, rocking her from side to side before she dropped a kiss on the child's dark hair.

"Mami Raina!"

"*Mija* Felipa!"

Devon's powerful arms encircled both of them, holding her family close. Raina praised God in her heart as she realized He had finally delivered the family of her dreams in a jungle village in Guatemala.

"I. Love. You," Felipa said in English.

Raina echoed her feelings in Spanish, thrilled that Greg and Caitlyn had worked with her daughter to learn a few words.

"Mi bonita mija," Devon whispered. "It's a little warm for such a long embrace."

At last, the three broke apart. Felipa jabbered in Spanish, leading Raina around the village. Raina caught enough words to understand.

They spent a wonderful evening together, giving Felipa a chance to say goodbye to her friends. They would be back next year, God willing, to serve together as a family.

In the morning, they would fly back to their brand new house on Vargas Ranch—so new, the landscaping still needed installed. Felipa would meet Abuelo John, her new grandfather. She and Devon moved him into the father-in-law suite at their house before the wedding a few days ago.

The wedding had been perfect. John walked her down the aisle and danced the father-daughter dance with her. Devon teared up during the vows, but repeated them flawlessly. For once, Raina's eyes remained dry. Greg and Caitlyn came up for the wedding, as Devon had asked Greg to be his best man.

In a few weeks, Devon would start his position as the full-time history teacher at Wickenburg High. He had subbed from February through the end of the school year, only learning the job was his a few weeks before the wedding.

She and Devon had also mapped out a new program at the ranch for foster kids in the area. Each of the school breaks, group homes would bus the kids in for a few days to stay in a new building near the bunkhouse. They planned to offer a variety of options, including working with the cattle, serving in the equine therapy program, horseback riding, basketball, tennis, and volleyball. Besides being a Radcliff for Felipa, she and Devon would be for so many kids from the local area. She could hardly wait.

Raina's heart filled to overflowing as Devon stood behind her, both watching Felipa play soccer with her friends.

He slathered some bug repellent on her arms before he wrapped his around her.

"So, is this an okay honeymoon?"

She smiled as she turned to face him, placing a hand on his soft beard. "Only the best."

Then he waggled his eyebrows before his lips captured hers, reminding her of the promise to love and cherish each other for the rest of their lives.

Continue the series with Drake's story in *Falling for a Humbug Cowboy (Vargas Ranch Book 5).*

From The Author

―――――――

When I first mapped out the Vargas Ranch Series, I always planned for Raina's character's back story as an orphan. I also planned the shocking family secret reveal for Devon.

But Devon threw me a few curveballs as I got to know his character better. I had no intention of writing about the mission trip until I started writing the book. Originally, I planned his need for a passport, and thus needing his birth certificate, for a trip to Europe to visit historic sites related to WWII. Although he loves history, I just couldn't see the servant-hearted Devon taking that trip.

The idea for a mission trip was inspired by one of my co-workers at the Christian ministry I work for. He was telling me about his mission trip to Ecuador a few years ago. That idea morphed when I modeled Devon's mission trip after a ministry dear to me, KidzAtHeart. They train missionaries specifically to reach children all over the world for Christ. I knew the founder back in the early 2000s through the Women's ministry at my church. After she passed away, her husband continued the ministry until his retirement in May 2024. The ministry is still thriving and equipping missionaries today. If you or someone you know is interested in following in Devon's footsteps by ministering to kids, please consider KidzAtHeart.

Thank you so much for your continued support. I hope you enjoyed Devon and Raina's story. Life never seems to go according to our plans, but God's plan is always the best, even when it hurts.

Watch for Drake's story in *Falling for a Humbug Cowboy (Vargas Book 5)*. It picks up Drake's story the day after the shocking family reveal—just in time for Christmas. The first Christmas he doesn't feel like celebrating.

Karen Baney

Find me on my website www.karenbaney.com, Book-Bub, Facebook, X, Instagram, or sign up for my newsletter for a free gift.

Books By Karen Baney

<u>Contemporary Romance</u>

<u>**Vargas Ranch Series:**</u>
Love is in the air at the Vargas Guest Ranch & Resort near Wickenburg, Arizona. The Vargas family lives and breathes their family motto: *We do not deviate from the Lord's plan.* Five brawny brothers keep the ranch and resort running while life lassos their hearts in this epic contemporary cowboy romance series.

Falling for a Real Cowboy | (A, E, P)
Falling for a Shy Cowboy | (A, E, P)
Falling for a Bossy Cowboy | (A, E, P)
Falling for a Smart Cowboy | (A, E, P)
Falling for a Humbug Cowboy – coming 2024
Falling for a Devoted Cowgirl – coming 2025
Falling for a Pregnant Cowgirl – coming 2025

<u>**Steadfast Love Series:**</u>
A group of friends learn to rely on God's steadfast love as they navigate life's ups and downs while finding romance in Chandler, Arizona.

The Heart I Rescue (prequel) | (A, E, P)
The Air I Breathe | (A, E, P)

<u>Historical Western Romance</u>

<u>**Prescott Pioneers Series:**</u>
The series is set in Prescott, Arizona between 1863 - 1870. Follow the lives of the Andersons, Colters, Larsons, Cahills, and Lancasters as they deal with heartache and hope for a new life in Arizona.

A Dream Unfolding | (A, E, P)
A Heart Renewed | (E, P)
A Life Restored | (E, P)

A Hope Revealed | (E, P)
Hidden Prospects | (E, P)

Desert Manna Series:
Follows the lives of three different couples as they trust God through tragedy, heartache, and restoration. Set in Prescott, Arizona between 1871 - 1873.

Beauty for Ashes | (E, P)
Joy for Mourning | (E, P)
Oaks of Justice | (E, P)

Colter Sons Series:
Coming of age stories about Will and Hannah Colter's five sons and their surprise daughter. Set in Prescott and other locations within the Arizona Territory in 1887 - 1906.

The Reluctant Cattleman | (A, E, P)
The Roaming Adventurer | (A, E, P)
The Railroad Magnate | (E, P)
The Resourceful Stockman | (E, P)
The Restless Wrangler | (E, P)
The Resilient Bride | (E, P)

Starry Night Novellas:
One starry night, three sisters pray for the man of their dreams. Caty dreams of a godly man who makes beautiful things from wood. Penny's heart belongs to Nathan Cahill. If only he felt the same. Dory longs for a man like her father. Set in Prescott, Arizona in 1886 - 1894.

Caty's Craftsman | (E, P)
Penny's Pursuit | (E, P)
Dory's Desire | (E, P)

A = Audiobook, E = eBook, P = Paperback